Cobalt City Dragonstorm

(A Cobalt City Universe Anthology)

Amanda Cherry, Nathan Crowder,
Erik Scott de Bie, Rosemary Jones,
and Dawn Vogel

Cover Art by Luke Spooner

Other Cobalt City Universe Stories

By Nathan Crowder
Greetings From Buena Rosa (2006, Timid Pirate Publishing)
Ride Like the Devil (2007, Timid Pirate Publishing; reprinted 2018, DefCon One Publishing)
Chanson Noir: Protectorate Vol. 1 (2009, Timid Pirate Publishing)
Cobalt City Blues: Protectorate Vol. 2 (2010, Timid Pirate Publishing)
Cobalt City: Los Muertos (2014)
Cobalt City: Ties that Bind (2015; reprinted 2018, DefCon One Publishing)
Cobalt City: Resistance (2018)
The Calling: Red Stag & the Wild Hunt Vol. 1 (2020)

By Amanda Cherry
Rites and Desires (2018, Def Con One Publishing)

By Erik Scott de Bie
Eye for an Eye (originally published as a part of *Cobalt City Double Feature*, 2012, Timid Pirate Publishing; reprinted 2018, DefCon One Publishing)

By Dawn Vogel
Sparx and Arrows (2016, DefCon One Publishing)
Coast to Coast Stars (2020, DefCon One Publishing)
Sure Shot in Las Capas: The Case of the Absent Star (2021, DefCon One Publishing)

By Jeremy Zimmerman
Kensei (originally published as a part of *Cobalt City Rookies*, 2012, Timid Pirate Publishing; reprinted 2014, DefCon One Publishing)
The Love of Danger (2015, DefCon One Publishing)
The Devil, You Say (2015, DefCon One Publishing)
Snowflake War Journal (2016, DefCon One Publishing)
Kensei Tales: Offensive Driving (2016, DefCon One Publishing)
Kensei Tales: It's the Great Yule Cat, Jamie Hattori (2016, DefCon One Publishing)
Kensei Tales: Live and In Concert (2017, DefCon One Publishing)
Kensei Tales: Unorthodoxy (2017, Def Con One Publishing)

Cobalt City Anthologies
Cobalt City Christmas (2009, Timid Pirate Publishing)
Cobalt City Timeslip (2010, Timid Pirate Publishing)
Cobalt City Dark Carnival (2011, Timid Pirate Publishing)
Cobalt City Double Feature (2012, Timid Pirate Publishing, featuring *Eye for an Eye* by Erik Scott de Bie and *The Place Between* by Minerva Zimmerman)
Cobalt City Rookies (2012, Timid Pirate Publishing, featuring *Tatterdemalion* by Nikki Burns, *Wrecker of Engines* by Rosemary Jones, and *Kensei* by Jeremy Zimmerman)
Cobalt City Christmas: Christmas Harder (2016)

CONTENTS

Prologue

by Nathan Crowder

The wind picked up an hour before sunset, worsening to a gale that stripped awnings from market stalls and toppled more than a few vendor carts, scattering their wares among the alleys and arcades. It had moved on to peeling loose clay tiles from the roofs of old buildings by the time lightning started less than an hour later. Anyone foolish or desperate enough to still be outside braving the scouring wind bore witness to the sky above the Grand Bazaar splitting open like an over-ripe melon to reveal a sea of unknown stars blazing yellow beyond.

From this portal floated the King in Yellow, graceful as a falling blossom despite his daunting stature. The wind died down as if in deference to the scion of madness, not even strong enough to ruffle the ivory veil suspended over his face by fine silver chains connected to the swept-back peak of his carved bone helm. Tiny charms danced playfully upon those silver chains. If anyone knew what the charms represented, that knowledge had driven them to madness.

Just to gaze upon the King in Yellow in his full glory was to be crushed by his enormous presence, to be driven to gibbering insanity by sheer weight of his wrongness. Bearing witness to the King in Yellow's arrival was a psychic trauma that broke most souls. And for any beings unfortunate enough to somehow withstand the assault, it meant a lifetime of devotion and obsession, forever doomed to try and seek out the king and his lost, fallen kingdom of Carcosa.

From the windows of his collection room, the blazing eyes of The Flame Who Fell from the Heavens watched the King in

Yellow's arrival. He curled his colossal, scaly red torso in barely repressed rage. His kind was made of stern stuff. In his centuries, he had witnessed things that would make gods weep and crumble. But even he dared not look upon the King in Yellow for long. He willed the glass pergola ceiling to open and flew out to meet his guest.

Standing somewhere in the vicinity of twelve to eighteen feet depending on how your brain perceived him, the King in Yellow looked small in comparison to the draconic-appearing form of The Flame Who Fell from the Heavens. Even so, the Master of the Grand Bazaar bowed his massive head in deference. "I had not thought you would come."

"Speak," the King in Yellow intoned, his voice like a powerful echo from miles away. "What grievance is so great that you would willingly invite madness to your world?"

"Your pet, Louis Malenfant," The Flame Who Fell from the Heavens said, spitting the occultist's name out as if it carried a bitter taste. "He dared to steal from me. I seek recompence."

"I will not give him to you," the King in Yellow said. "Not out of loyalty to him, of course. But he is beyond my reach. But surely there is some other way I can settle his debt."

"Return what he stole from me, and it shall be forgiven," The Flame Who Fell from the Heavens said, perhaps a bit too boldly, as he immediately recoiled, anticipating a harsh response. With a more conciliatory tone, he added, "The Albion Codex was a gem in my collection. Its value is beyond emeralds and rubies to me."

The wind picked up briefly, rippling the King in Yellow's long robes. For just a second, the veil shifted over his face, and though The Flame Who Fell from the Heavens saw only a fraction of the face beneath for the briefest of seconds, it was a sight that would remain a scar on his brain for the remainder of his very long life.

"There are others of you, yes?" The King in Yellow said. "Other ... dragons? Do you have any influence over them?"

One huge, blazing eye narrowed in skepticism. "Many others, scattered among the stars and the Coil itself. I would not claim influence, but my voice does carry certain weight. Why do you ask?"

"I will not give you Louis Malenfant, but there are other manners in which to seize your revenge. I will provide you the coordinates to his world—the world he foolishly seeks to preserve

2

with his current rebellious streak. Summon your kind and wreak havoc upon Cobalt City. You wish to destroy Louis Malenfant? Then destroy that which he loves."

It wasn't what he sought, but it was good. The way to Cobalt City, to Iteration 5169, had been lost to his kind for some time now. It would be a pleasure to feast upon their fear again. But The Flame Who Fell from the Heavens was first and foremost a merchant, and a canny one at that. The deal was too good. "And how does this benefit you, may I ask?"

The King in Yellow laughed, and the sound bore into the souls of every person who heard it for half a mile in every direction. They would hear that laugh in their nightmares for years. "Need you even ask? Their modern world has no place for dragons. A storm of dragons descending upon the city, taking root, bringing primal fears to life? It will be utter madness. And in that madness, I find opportunity. Do your part, and you can strip the meat from the carcass of that world. And when you're done, I shall claim its soul."

Facing the Music

by Amanda Cherry

Ruby Kilingsworth didn't bother looking up from her laptop screen when she heard the unannounced, uninvited visitor let themself into her private office. Interruptions were irksome always, but never more so than when she'd chosen to work from the office in her penthouse rather than the one several floors down in the Goblin Records corporate suite.

"Learn to knock," she snapped.

"No."

Had any other voice given that reply, its owner would have been made to sorely regret it. But it wasn't just anyone's voice. For a moment, she wasn't sure she'd heard correctly, and when she looked up, there was a moment when she could barely believe her eyes.

The god of mischief was standing not ten feet away from her, smirking as he slowly sashayed toward her desk.

"Not who I was expecting to see," Ruby said, as though it was somehow less than obvious.

"You're expecting someone?" Loki asked. "Because if you are, you should call them and cancel."

"No," she answered, "I'm not. What I meant was: *you* are unexpected. This is not a room in which I might expect to see you. In fact, this is a room in which I expect to see practically no one. I come up here so I can work in peace."

"Wait," Loki said, "You're ... working?" His face screwed itself into an expression like he had just smelled something foul

"This is an office, Loki."

5

"Sure it is," he allowed, "but I figured it was just aesthetic. I can't imagine you actually doing work."

"Media empires don't run themselves, you know. I might make it look easy, but I assure you it is not."

"Sounds ghastly."

"Well then, darling," Ruby replied, "if you're so allergic to work, why the hell did you barge into my office?" Ruby closed her laptop and folded her hands on her desk. "Not that I so much care, but usually when someone interrupts my workday, they have a damn good reason for it. I'm on tenterhooks wanting to know what can't wait 'til after hours."

"I need you."

"An unusual request for the middle of a weekday," she answered, "and one I'm going to have to postpone satisfying, I'm afraid."

"I didn't mean it that way," he replied. "I mean I need your help."

"Well, you're just full of surprises, aren't you?" Ruby shook her head and leaned back I her chair, crossing her arms over her chest as she did. "And while I'm not making any promises of actual assistance, I am curious to know what you need my help *with*."

"A dragon."

"Come again?"

"I need your help with a dragon."

"Only you." Ruby sighed. She put her fingers to her temples and shook her head for a moment before looking back at her guest and adding, "Tell me more. What about a dragon?"

"Fafnir," Loki said. His tone said Ruby should absolutely know what he was talking about. She did not.

"Fafnir," she repeated as she attempted to plumb the depths of her memory for why that name seemed familiar.

"Fafnir."

Ruby recalled after a moment. "The dragon you slayed."

Loki nodded. "Except for the fact he's immortal, so the slaying was ... eh."

"Right, right. It's coming back to me." Ruby drummed her fingers against the arms of her chair as she worked to remember the context of her familiarity with this story. "This was the whole business in Bayreuth, yes?"

"Indeed."

"I seem to recall we'd taken care of that," she said. "We enchanted an opera."

"We did enchant an opera," he replied. "But—"

Ruby did not like the sound of that. "But?"

"It seems there's a bit of a snag," Loki said. "A complication, as it were."

"What the hell could be complicated?" Ruby asked, not even trying to hide her annoyance. "As I recall, that magic was perfectly straightforward. And brilliant, if I do say so myself. Am I missing something? Because the way I understand it, every time some unsuspecting divo sings the enchanted lyrics while plunging his make-believe sword into the big dragon puppet, the real dragon gets a real poke in the guts. He stays wounded, you get unfettered access to whatever it is he has that you want. Is that not what we made happen, or has it somehow stopped working?"

"My plan was brilliant," Loki said, "and our magic was flawless. It's been fine for years now."

"So again, I ask: what is the problem?"

"Technically two problems."

"All right," Ruby replied. "What are the *two* problems?"

"Problem number one is that the opera world has hit a bit of a slump."

"Slump?"

"Worse than slump," Loki asserted, "rising to the level of complete cultural atrophy."

"And by that you mean?" There were times when Ruby could abide Loki's monologuing—times when she enjoyed it, even. But at this moment, she really needed him to get to the point.

"I mean no one's performing *Siegfried*," he spat. "No one. Not one damn company in almost two years."

"Well that can't be true," Ruby said. "Even if no one else is producing Wagner, the Bayreuth Festival is on stage every year. That's what made the whole thing so brilliant."

"Until the Bayreuth opera house got water damaged and needed a major renovation."

"What?"

"They've ripped the whole place down to studs," Loki replied. "It's a three-year project. There was no *Ring* cycle last year, none this year, and there isn't one scheduled for next year, either."

"And am I to take it from your level of panic that it's also not on any other company's schedule?"

"Correct."

"And as a result, you're about to have a problem with a dragon."

"We," Loki corrected her. "We are about to have a problem with a dragon."

"Oh, no," Ruby countered. "This one's all you, darling. Seeing as I have no interest in looting the hoard of an incapacitated lizard of size, I honestly don't give a damn if he's suddenly no longer incapacitated."

"You really should, you know."

"And why is that?"

"Because your magic's all over the rite that's kept him down. When he comes looking to get his revenge, you'll be just as high on his smiting list as I am."

"While I am all for a proper smiting every now and again," Ruby replied, "I will remind you that the dragon in question cannot enter the mortal realm. As long as I don't go venturing through the Coil, I'll be perfectly safe—a tack I might recommend to you as well, at least until the next production of *Siegfried* goes up."

"You think Fafnir can't reach you here?"

"I know he can't. It's impossible."

"Says the inhumanly powerful sorceress to the god who's come to call without need of an avatar."

"Touché," Ruby replied. She stood from her desk and walked around to lean against the far side. "And as much as I wouldn't put it past you to dangle the threat of a dragonly smiting as a means to manipulate me into helping you, that doesn't feel like what's going on here."

"Oh, it's not," Loki assured her.

"What do you know that I don't?" she asked pointedly. "What has you so scared?"

"There's something going on," Loki answered.

"Something?" Ruby rolled her eyes as she shook her head. This was not the time for vagaries, but since when had Loki ever given a straightforward answer?

"I don't know ... exactly," he admitted. "But I know it has to do with the King in Yellow, and I know there's about to be a whole mess of dragons on this side of the Coil."

"The King in Yellow?"

"Mm-hmmm."

"I suppose if anyone could—"

"Indeed."

"And should I ask how you wound up privy to this information?"

"You could ask, but—"

"But nothing," Ruby interrupted him. "You were probably tickled at the impending mayhem until you realized one of these rampaging dragons might be coming for you personally."

"I will neither confirm nor deny my initial support of the concept," Loki replied. But his smirk told Ruby everything she needed to know.

"Of course not," she said.

"Suffice to say I know what's coming, and what's coming is an invasion of dragons the likes of which the mortal realm has never even imagined."

"And you'd prefer the dragon who's mad at you not be among them," Ruby added.

"You as well," he surmised.

Ruby stood up straight and shook her head. This was a bigger problem than she'd dealt with in quite a while, and being no particular expert on dragons, she wasn't really sure where to begin. "So did you come here with a plan?" she asked, hoping the god in her office might have thought things through already. "Or are we starting from scratch?"

"The solution is obvious." Loki leaned back against the arm of the chair, kicked his legs, and threw his arms out to his sides. With as wicked a grin as Ruby had ever seen cross his face, he wiggled his fingers and announced, "Let's put on a show!"

~

Loki hadn't been kidding.

His best, and only, idea was for Ruby to use her not-insubstantial fortune and influence to make a production of *Siegfried* happen as soon as was humanly possible. Sooner, he hoped, than the King in Yellow could bring his own plan to fruition. Once again hobbling the dragon in question should at least protect them from the worst of what was to come.

As much as Ruby hated to admit, it wasn't a bad idea. In fact, it was one of the more clever plots she'd ever known Loki to concoct. If the only sure way to keep a dragon who might mean her harm from passing through the Coil to seek vengeance was to get an opera onstage, then that's precisely what Ruby Killingsworth was going to do.

Putting the pieces together had proven easier than anticipated.

As had been the case for most of Ruby's career in entertainment, a smattering of magic along with the liberal application cash money had been enough to grease even the squeakiest of operatic wheels.

Honestly, the hardest part had been getting the Maestro from Bayreuth on the phone to begin with.

She knew first-hand, from her days of touring with musicians, that putting up a show was far too complex a process to work in the time Loki figured they had. But she also knew that picking up an existing show and plopping it down in a new venue was markedly less difficult. So it hadn't taken long for her to figure out an angle.

Calling it a "cultural exchange," she'd talked the folks in Bayreuth into packing their whole kit and caboodle and bringing it to Cobalt City for a two-night run of *Siegfried*. It had taken some work to get them to understand that when she'd said "unlimited budget," she'd really meant *unlimited* budget, but once it set in that money was really no object, they'd been happy to work with her.

Not surprising for an organization faced with three years without revenue and the bill for a major renovation.

And the Maestro had been almost giddy when he'd called to let Ruby know they would have his first choice in the leading role, a certain up-and-coming tenor named Torvald Fuchs who was making waves in the international opera scene. Just off an award-winning run of *La Fille du Regiment*, he was by all accounts an exceedingly handsome, exceptionally talented star in the making who commanded a pay rate that could bring the average company manager to tears.

Ruby Killingsworth was not the average company manager.

She'd been more than happy to cover his pay and that of any other top talent if it meant getting the show up and running on the dates they'd chosen.

Barely three weeks had passed between Loki's showing up in Ruby's office and the day the opera was being loaded into Cobalt City's Liberty Theater.

Less than one week later, the curtain was about to go up.

Wearing a pewter-colored A-line gown with hand-stitched beaded lace and a scandalously low-cut bodice, Ruby couldn't help her smile as she wound her way through the opening night crowd. With only a few weeks in which to promote the production, there hadn't been a lot of optimism in regard to ticket sales. Tonight's capacity crowd was quite the welcome surprise.

Apparently Torvald Fuchs had a following among a certain set of young Manhattanites desperate to give the impression they appreciated opera. Ruby hated that kind of pretension, but she was glad to take their money anyway.

She almost wished she'd set the ticket price higher.

Not that this production could ever have found its way into the black. Between the enormous cargo jet she'd had to charter to bring in the set, the salaries of the performers and musicians, and the three full crews of union stagehands she'd hired to ensure the show could be loaded in and ready for curtain on time, Ruby had spent herself tidily into the "loss" column. And that was before having to pay off the Liberty's would-be renters to change their date or venue so they could have the theater for the time they needed.

It had taken a huge expenditure of both time and money to make this thing happen.

No matter.

The theater was sold out and that was enough to call it a success. The not-insubstantial tax deduction would make the net loss more than worth it in the long run. Especially considering this whole thing was only a pretense through which to work a bit of magic and keep a dragon off her ass.

It was a bonus that the Liberty's facilities people had welcomed pieces from Ruby's *private collection* to decorate the lobby in the ambiance of the production. It was the temporary relocation of a few particular artifacts that made it possible for Loki to join her in her box for the show. Dressed in an exquisite brocade waistcoat and tails, he looked every bit the part of a nouveau-riche dandy as he sat on the edge of his chair and watched the curtain rise, visibly ecstatic at once again seeing his opera magic live and on stage.

Whatever fuss the tabloids made about the tall stranger sitting with Miss Killingsworth at the opera would be tomorrow's problem. Tonight was for slaying dragons.

And a hearty slaying it was sure to be.

Torvald Fuchs had proven himself to be every bit worth the hype—and the expense. He was an astonishingly handsome beefcake of a man with a voice so robust and angelic that Ruby had made a point of sitting in on his last few rehearsals. She'd also had him over for dinner and ... extracurricular activities—a few times, in fact.

And with a sold-out theater to play to, he once again did not disappoint.

His performance of the Forging song at the end of the first act had even Loki out of his seat to applaud.

As the lights flashed to signal the end of the first intermission, Ruby couldn't have been more content. The musicians were brilliant, the production was gorgeous, the champagne was flowing, and she knew her mood would only improve with the next few movements.

But 45 minutes into the second act, as the lights came up on the entrance to the cave, Ruby realized something had gone horribly, terrifyingly wrong.

"Fuck." Ruby grabbed Loki by his arm as she sprang forward in her seat. She put her opera glasses to her face, looking closely at the stage to be sure her eyes weren't deceiving her.

"What?" he asked. "What is it? What's wrong?"

Ruby stood from her seat then, yanking Loki from his with the death-grip she still held on his arm. Her eyes were *not* deceiving her. This was bad.

"That's not the puppet," she whispered harshly as she dragged him through the curtain separating the box seats from the mezzanine lobby.

"What?"

"That's. Not. The puppet!" she repeated, louder this time now that they were out of earshot of the rest of the auditorium. Ruby snatched up as much of her skirt as would fit in one hand and took off running toward the stairs down to the stage level.

"Yes, yes, I heard you say that," Loki replied, doing his best to keep up. "I understood the words just fine. But now you've got to tell me what they mean."

"I mean what's on the stage right now is not the fucking dragon puppet they imported from Bayreuth," she replied curtly, tossing a glower over her shoulder at him as she continued down the stairs. "I mean I was here yesterday to watch Torvald learn the blocking with the dragon; I have seen the puppet and that is not it."

"So you think—?"

"You're damn right that's what I think," Ruby spat. "What the hell else could it be?" She let go of him then, gathering more of her skirt in her arms as she sped down the mezzanine stairs and through the door labeled "Authorized Personnel Only".

The stage manager looked up as Ruby burst into the backstage with Loki hot on her heels. Ruby could tell she was about to shoo them away but stopped short when she recognized the intruder as the opera's executive producer. Attending those rehearsals was proving to have been an excellent decision.

The show was still going on, and Ruby turned her attention to the stage just in time to see the dragon's eyes come open. He growled then, plumes of steam wafting from his nostrils as Torvald Fuchs continued to sing. On cue with the music, the dragon opened his mouth, baring rows of opalescent teeth as his human voice sounded via the house speakers.

For a moment, Ruby thought maybe everything would be ok. Maybe she'd been wrong to jump to the conclusion she had. Maybe this was just a much-improved version of the puppet—a result of the overnight efforts of numerous highly-skilled stagehands.

For another few measures, the scene went on as intended, and Ruby began to let herself relax. But Torvald was barely into the next phrase before the dragon lunged forward, snapping up the sword-wielding tenor with its mighty jaws and lifting him up off the stage.

Ruby screamed.

Loki grabbed her by the arm as he stumbled backward, nearly pulling both of them off-balance as the stage manager brushed past them, running full-speed into the wings to get a closer look at what was happening.

The audience reaction was mixed, and noisy. Some people were cheering what they must have thought an extraordinary feat of animatronics. Others—likely those more familiar with the opera—cried out in obvious horror at the carnage before them.

Even over the sound of the orchestra, Ruby could hear the crunching of bones as Fafnir threw his head back and chomped down on the handsome tenor between his jaws, leaving only a pair of leather boots visible through his teeth.

The music was getting quieter, beginning to wane; Ruby snapped her head around to look at the Maestro in the pit. His face had gone ashen, and he stood frozen on his podium as the musicians began to realize they were no longer being conducted.

Ruby had to think fast. She had to do something about the dragon and also something to keep the audience from erupting in complete pandemonium.

Looking around for a solution to present itself, Ruby spotted the cables to the theater's fire curtain. Using a small but mighty burst of magic, she sliced through the lot of them, causing the curtain to fall abruptly from its overhead rig. An opaque fiberglass barrier between their seats carnage on the stage should handle the audience for now.

"What the hell?" the stage manager screamed.

"I need the understudy," Ruby replied, taking the woman by her shoulders and putting enough magic behind that order to make certain it would be followed without question.

The stage manager, having no real choice in the matter, stumbled back to her podium and picked up her headset.

"What are you thinking?" Loki asked, slinking farther into the wings. "What are we going to do?"

Ruby wasn't sure. She hadn't gotten that far yet. All she knew for certain was that the dragon Fafnir was there in the flesh and their only hope of putting him down was the magic in the music—so no matter what else happened, they had to get through the scene.

Ruby was looking impatiently toward the dressing room door when her eyes landed on three plastic swords sitting on a backstage table, all of them identical to the one now residing in the dragon's gullet alongside the late Torvald Fuchs.

She grabbed Loki's wrist and pulled him behind her as she dashed toward the table.

"We have to slay it," she said, reaching out to take one of the prop swords from the table.

"With a plastic sword?" His voice sounded louder than it had a moment ago, and Ruby realized it was because the last of the instruments had finally stopped playing, leaving the sound of the dragon's mastication to echo unaccompanied through the auditorium.

This was bad.

Sword still in hand, Ruby ran to the stage manager's podium.

"You have to tell him to keep playing!" she said. "Keep the music going. Take it back to the top of the scene."

"But—" the stage manager began.

Ruby shook her head. There was no time for "but".

The stage manager nodded, clicking the button to talk into her headset as a young man approached her from behind.

"You called me," he said to the stage manager.

She nodded and pointed to Ruby. "Talk to the EP!" she replied, her hand over the mic on her headset.

The young man nodded and turned to Ruby. "Ma'am," he said.

Ruby looked the lad up and down and frowned. He was a *child*. Young, blonde, willowy—gangly by some standards—the fellow in no way resembled Torvald Fuchs. Ruby would not for a minute have bought him as Siegfried. But this was one of those rare occasions when even Ruby Killingsworth couldn't afford to be choosy.

If he could sing the part, then he would just have to do.

"I need you to go on," she said to him.

"Ma'am?"

"You heard me. You're Siegfried now; go sing."

The understudy shook his head. "I'm not dressed. I'm not warmed up—"

"Now ask me if I care," Ruby replied. "No. Wait. Don't. No time for that." Sword still in hand, she grabbed the singer by his arm and marched him into the first wing, downstage of the fire curtain.

"What's going on?" he asked, his voice betraying clear panic and confusion as he gestured to the deployed fire curtain.

Ruby could tell he had no idea what was happening on the stage, and she figured it was best to keep it that way. The plan she was hatching was contingent on his ability to sing the enchanted movement without error. Letting on that there was a chance he, too, could wind up between a dragon's jaws would not have been helpful.

"I assure you," Ruby replied, "you don't want to know." She shook her head as she looked down at the visibly bewildered Maestro in the pit, his baton raised to restart the orchestra just as soon as everyone was done turning back their pages.

"I—"

"You are going to sing this scene. Don't worry about wardrobe. Don't worry about props. Don't worry about blocking. You'll stand on the apron, keep your eyes on the conductor, and you'll fucking sing. What you will *not* do," Ruby added, "is pay any attention—any attention at all—to the sounds on the stage behind you."

"There's trouble with the puppet," Loki called out, ostensibly to help. "It ... um ... it injured the other guy. That's' why we need you."

"Oh, no!" the understudy replied. "Is he ok?"

Ruby was not prepared to answer that. "Let us worry about Torvald and the dragon. You worry about giving this audience the best damn Siegfried you possibly can."

"Forest Murmurs" began to play. The conductor had done as requested; they were back at the top of the scene. There was no more time for convincing this kid to get his scrawny ass out on stage. Ruby had hoped the lad would be excited to go on, as understudies tend to be. His hesitation was frustrating. Was she really going to have to use magic for this?

Right as she was preparing to bodily shove the understudy out onto the apron, she discovered she didn't need to. Still in sweatpants and sneakers, he emerged onto the stage and caught the eye of the Maestro.

"Okay," Ruby said then, turning to Loki and walking upstage, "we're going to get our magic music."

"Good," Loki replied. "Right. Yes." He stopped short of following her into the third wing and put his hands on his hips. "But I think you're still missing a major point here."

"And what's that?" Ruby asked, certain she had not missed anything, but curious as to what he thought she was doing.

"The magic in the music will almost certainly work," he said, "but that's still a fake sword. And, magic music or no, I don't think a fake sword is going to do much against a real dragon."

"How about in the hands of a real god?" she rebutted, shoving the plastic sword into Loki's arms. "You want that tin sword to be made of iron, you make it that way. I will do everything I can to keep the dragon's attention on me. Then you sneak the hell up and you stab him. Got it?"

She didn't have time to wait for an answer.

The horn-call had sounded, signaling the beginning of the enchanted section. If they wanted the music to work with them, they only had a few minutes to get this dragon slain.

Having finally swallowed Torvald Fuchs, Fafnir roared. Sonorous and terrifying, the noise cut through the sound of the French horn and the still-mumbling audience.

As Ruby looked across the stage, she caught a glimpse of the terrified fellow who was set to sing the dragon's part. He was quaking in his velvet loafers in the stage left wings, holding onto his headphones and shaking his head at his video monitor. He seemed to be aware of what had just happened on stage, and Ruby realized he might be the only other person in the theater to understand what was really going on.

She didn't let herself wonder what had become of the puppeteers.

The low bass of Fafnir's human voice rang out across the auditorium—the singer in the opposite wing having turned back to his microphone and monitor. Ruby wasn't sure she had ever been so relieved at anyone's deciding just to do their damn job.

"It's now or never," Ruby said.

But Loki seemed to know that already. He stalked onto the stage, obviously terrified but also determined. The sword in his hand had already begun to transform—gaining heft and sharpness as he grew nearer to the dragon.

Ruby followed, unsure of what she ought to do next.

Combat magic had never been her forte. In fact, for most of her life she hadn't even been capable of it. She was much more likely to use her magic to make a hasty exit when violence was threatening. But the powers she'd gained from her time with the Eye of Africa were different. There was more to her now, and she suspected she was about to learn just how much.

She'd toyed with these magicks a few times; she knew she could put a man down if she needed to.

A dragon, though? That was likely to prove a challenge. But it wasn't like she was in this on her own.

She'd put that sword in Loki's hand for a reason. He'd been the one to dispatch this beast in the first place, and it had been his scheming that got them into this whole mess to begin with.

She could only hope he knew what he was doing.

Either way, she'd know soon enough. Ruby watched as Loki got closer, waiting for the moment Fafnir became aware of his presence.

That moment wasn't hard to spot. Fafnir craned his neck, tilting his head down to regard the sword-wielding trickster approaching from the wings. His eyes narrowed and another plume of steam escaped his nostrils along with a mighty rumble. He knew what was happening, he knew what he'd come for, and by Ruby's best estimation, he knew who he was up against.

This wasn't going to be easy.

Ruby looked quickly back and forth between the dragon and the fiberglass fire curtain separating them from the singers and the audience. Whether or not this dragon could breathe fire remained to be seen, but in case he could, having put a fireproof layer between him and the audience would prove beneficial.

It was likely she'd know any minute.

Before Fafnir had the chance to snap, Ruby let out a blast from her hands: an orange-gold flash of heat and shock that hit the dragon squarely in the head. The magic knocked him backward, but he recovered quickly, rearing up onto his hind legs and letting out the most horrible, screeching roar Ruby had ever heard.

"What the hell?" Loki yelled over his shoulder. "You made it mad!"

"It was already mad!"

"Well, now it's madder!"

"You remember how to do this, right?" Ruby asked then, realizing maybe she should have asked before getting the dragon's attention.

"Kind of."

"The fuck is kind of?"

"It's been a while!"

"Just follow the script," she reminded him. "Stab it in the heart. A couple of times if you can."

Loki charged forward like a possessed creature: sword pointed up from the end of his outstretched arm as he ran full-bore toward the still-wailing dragon.

Ruby winced; that wasn't exactly what she'd meant. But he was about to make contact anyway. Loki closed the distance quickly, but Fafnir swatted the sword from his hand before coming at him with teeth bared and jaws agape.

Ruby quickly hurled another burst of magic in his direction.

Her second casting hit the beast in almost the same place as the first, but she could tell immediately it hadn't had the same effect. Fafnir's head was knocked sideways, but he stood fast. He quickly snapped his head back again, this time taking a lumbering step toward Ruby.

Loki scrambled to recover the sword from the far wing, but the dragon seemed to pay him no mind, focused instead on the sorceress whose relentless barrage of castings had already left him with visible damage to the scales on his face.

Good. That was the point. Keep the dragon's attention away from the sword that was coming to deal its end.

The dragon continued to advance toward her, trampling over and tearing through the imaginary forest of the opera set, its massive foreclaws leaving divots in the stage as it came. The bony spikes on its head knocked into the hanging stage lights, shattering glass and bulbs and causing sparks to rain down onto the stage.

Fafnir lunged, opening his jaws wide as he came at Ruby with another piercing roar. Ruby moved to dodge but wound up tangled in the fabric of her skirt. She ducked as best she could while sending up a burst of magic to shield herself from the jagged teeth. The shield was enough; it stopped the massive jaws from closing around her, but Ruby could tell Fafnir was *pissed*.

As the dragon roared its discontent, she scooted herself across the floor into the mass of fake trees stage right of center. She got to her feet and took a deep breath in an attempt to center herself. She was coming to understand how egregiously she'd underestimated the amount of energy these castings would require. And things were just getting started. She'd need to pace herself if she was going to keep this up.

She was sore all over, and not just from flinging herself to the ground, although that certainly hadn't helped the situation. She'd hit the deck hard, but she hadn't been eaten, so that was a victory; it would be an awfully short-lived one if she couldn't keep the magic up.

A few more centering breaths later, Ruby reached around a burlap tree trunk and threw magic again, a burst of light this time, with only enough power and flash to blind her enemy for a moment while she moved to take better cover behind the mountain of prop gold on the far side of the stage. As she went, she spotted a stray leather boot lying on the stage deck—perhaps all that was left of Torvald Fuchs.

Pity. That fellow had real star potential. And he wasn't bad in the sack, either. But this was no time for mourning a lost opportunity for sex.

The dragon was looking for her, stomping its feet and spewing steam from its nostrils. Ruby peeked out just long enough to see Loki coming at Fafnir again, sword grasped tightly as he scurried toward the unsuspecting dragon.

Fafnir must have felt Loki's footfalls against the hollow stage deck. He turned suddenly, splaying his legs wide as Loki sped toward him. Just as Fafnir's gaze fell on the trickster god, Loki dropped to the deck, sliding beneath the dragon's chest and stabbing upward toward the shining scales of his underside.

Loki's sword found purchase, piercing the dragon where the silver scales of his neck began to meld with the darker ones on his chest.

Fafnir cried out, a fearsome rumble with the high-pitched undertone of a furious raptor. He lifted his front leg, swiping his giant claws squarely at Loki, this time clearly not aiming just to knock away the sword.

Ruby cast again, another blast of heat and force, this one directed straight at Fafnir's outstretched claws. But her spell flew wide, missing the beast's swinging arm and instead smashing the tangle of fake trees she'd been hiding behind just a few moments ago.

Even though it missed its target, the spell did its job, stopping the dragon mid-swipe with a barrage of shrapnel from the destroyed opera set. Fafnir turned again, sword still stuck in his chest, to roar back at Ruby. His jerking movement caused Loki to lose his grip on the sword. He rolled out from beneath Fafnir's belly, panting as the dragon reared back, both of its front legs off the ground as though he meant to crush Loki beneath his weight.

Ruby scrambled up the hill of false gold she'd been hiding behind, using magic to fling the sword out of the dragon's flesh and onto the floor beside Loki. He snatched it up immediately, scowling at the feeling of the sticky blood on the handle as he prepared to go in for another strike.

Ruby's next bit of magic was more her usual speed—a control spell. Trying new things against the dragon had worked with varying degrees of success, but it was time to pull out something a bit more familiar.

A lasso of visible light and debris formed around the dragon's neck, searing his scales with its heat and cutting into his flesh with its force. The smell was terrible, but for the first time tonight, Ruby felt like she had the upper hand. She tugged on the end of the magical binding, snapping Fafnir's head backward as Loki once again lunged forward with the sword.

Fafnir thrashed and jerked, screeching and snarling and pawing at the spectral rope as though his claws could break it. And maybe they could have. But Ruby held tight, concentrating on both her corporeal and her arcane grip on the dragon as Loki dodged the flailing claws, angling for a shot at the creature's heart.

Loki thrust the sword into the dragon's belly. Once, then again, and again, leaning in with his whole body as blood poured from the new wounds and the one he'd made earlier, dousing his face and his suit with vile black-red gore.

He was stabbing wildly, jabbing his weapon in between the angry dragon's scales at every angle possible. Still holding tight to the magical line around Fafnir's neck, Ruby was tempted to ask Loki if he was sure he remembered where this dragon kept its heart when she began to notice a change in their foe.

Fafnir's scales—dark, green, and iridescent—were beginning to flicker, to lighten, to take on hues as though they were reflecting some light from the theater's wings that Ruby was sure weren't actually there.

"What the—?"

"I got it!" Loki replied. Not that she'd been asking him, but Ruby understood immediately what he'd meant.

The dragon was shimmering, fading; he was coming in and out of focus, changing colors, and in places becoming almost translucent for moments at a time. His roars grew softer—not lessening in intensity and not changing pitch—but rather becoming muffled, as though the source of the din was much farther afield.

The strain against the confining spell lessened appreciably, although the dragon's thrashing and fighting was as fierce and as violent as ever. Whatever was happening, it was bigger than just this opera stage. And it was happening fast—a good thing as far as Ruby was concerned. She was sweating, her arms trembling from the struggle of immortal beast against magical restraint, and her heart racing such that she couldn't completely catch her breath.

The dragon flickered and faded, all the while trying to swipe away its magical bindings and to fend off the sword being continually shoved into his flesh. His appearance continued to waver and dim, until eventually Fafnir had disappeared altogether, leaving behind only smears of blood and the smashed remnants of the puppet that had once been staged in the place he'd occupied.

Ruby didn't want to think about what that thing was going to cost to repair.

"Is he—?" she asked, still out of breath.

"I don't know," Loki panted, "but he's gone for now and that's good enough."

"But you got him."

"I did. I just don't know how much or how well."

"I think we'll know that tomorrow," Ruby replied as she began to climb down from the hill of false gold, wiping the perspiration from her forehead with the back of her hand as she went.

"What do you mean?"

"I mean when this scene happens tomorrow, we can only hope to see that puny little understudy tilting at a puppet. The magic's intact," she reminded him, "so whatever happens on this stage tomorrow is only going to add to the damage we dealt tonight. We should be good—for a while anyway."

"You really think there'll be a performance tomorrow?" Loki asked, gesturing vaguely to the mess they'd left on the stage.

Ruby crossed her arms and frowned.

"I forget you've never seen me at work before," she replied. Ruby left the stage deck then, heading into the wings toward the shellshocked stage manager who was still sitting, white-knuckled, at her podium.

"Uhhh—" The stage manager looked up, but seemed unable to form words.

Ruby didn't care. "Tell the Maestro to keep playing," she said, adding just enough magic to the order to be sure it would overpower whatever else was happening in the poor woman's head. "Put Mime and Alberich out on the apron with Siegfried the scrawny and let them sing the rest of the second act from there. Then get the crew out here and get the set changed. Skip the second intermission and pick up at the top of Act Three like nothing went wrong."

The stage manager nodded, wide-eyed.

"Now!" Ruby added. That seemed to snap her out of her torpor.

"Yes ma'am," she replied, giving one last nod as she turned her attention back to the libretto on her podium and the switch on her headset.

"They're going to do the rest of the show?" Loki asked, approaching Ruby from behind as he watched the stage crew dash about, striking the remnants of the ruined set. "And you honestly think they can have things back together in time for curtain tomorrow night? And that it's going to go up like nothing ever happened?"

"Really, darling," Ruby said, patting down the frizz she could already feel forming in her sweat-dampened hair, "I thought you knew better by now than to underestimate me. By the time these people leave here tonight, all they'll remember of the last twenty minutes will be a minor technical difficulty and an aria sung in front of a curtain. If I can get my act together, they might not even remember that."

"What do you mean?"

"I mean I have the whole third act to fix the memories of these people."

"You think that'll work?"

"Again with the underestimations," Ruby chided. "I damn well know it'll work. And so will all three of the crews I've hired—right up until the first intermission tomorrow if they have to—to get some semblance of a forest put together and to either reassemble that mess of pieces into a passable dragon puppet or source me something new."

"Is that even possible?"

"You bet your ass it is. These people are professionals," she said, gesturing vaguely to the scrambling stagehands working to get the smashed cave set off the deck and Brunhilde's mountain on stage in its place.

"I don't doubt that," he replied, "but still—"

"But nothing," Ruby interrupted. "There is one truth universally acknowledged in this business, Loki. I thought you'd been around enough to know by now."

"Oh?" he asked. "And what's that?"

Ruby shook her head as she grinned back at him. "Silly darling," she said. "Haven't you heard? The show must go on."

———

Amanda Cherry is a Seattle-area queer, disabled nerd who still can't believe people pay her to write stories. Her debut novel, *Rites & Desires*, was released in 2018, and her sophomore work, *The Dragon Stone Conspiracy*, in 2021. She's had short stories published in *Cobalt City Christmas: Christmas Harder*, *Mad Scientist Journal*, and the queer sci-fi anthology, *Ink*. Amanda was on the writing team for the TTRPG *Acute Paranoia* and is an award-winning screenwriter. Her nonfiction writing has appeared across the web on such sites as ToscheStation.net, ElevenThirtyEight.com, and StarTrek.com. Amanda is a member of SFWA and Broad Universe and is represented by Claire Draper of the Bent Agency.

Paper Dragons, Electric Wings

by Rosemary Jones

Lizzie hummed along with the song audible only to her, all about paper wings, paper kisses, and a broken paper heart under a paper moon. It seemed appropriate for sorting through the books left behind by the students in odd spots around the library. Lizzie loved this Saturday morning job, roaming up and down the aisles, pushing her book cart before her, collecting the books abandoned everywhere except the shelves marked "leave books here for reshelving."

College students did not seem keen to read instructions. Lizzie smiled and shook her head at the neatly labeled but clearly bare shelf. Perhaps they believed hiding the books in various corners would make them more accessible next time, she thought, as she crawled under one study carrel desk to retrieve a stack of economic textbooks, a play about the women of Russian fairy tales, and an unopened package of Kit Kats. Food was not allowed in the library. Lizzie felt no guilt about confiscating them for sharing later in the librarian's lounge. She dropped the marvelous candy treat into the pocket of her velvet vest.

Lizzie's other college student job was serving coffee in the Student Union. She loved that job, too, but the student manager, Hank, complained to the staff supervisor about working with her.

"It's the way she makes coffee. It's weird. Look I don't mind her always being dressed in her steampunk cosplay outfits," she'd overheard him say to Iris Gunderson, the head of Food Service. "The customers think it's cute. Some of the other baristas started wearing their costumes to work too. One day we had a Stardust, Wrecker of Engines, and Lady Vengeance serving during her shift."

Lizzie smiled when she heard that. The Stardust and Lady Vengeance had been a couple of fans in their own fantastic interpretations of the superhero outfits. But the Wrecker of Engines had been real. Morgan Lee wanted to see what it was like working as a barista. Training for some undercover Wrecker op, according to him. She liked to think he wanted to spend more time with her before he left Cobalt City again for wherever he needed to go next. Being a hacker superhero led him to strange places far away, so different from her own journey from nowhere real to being grounded in this city.

Miss Gunderson, the gentle voiced African American woman who always tried to find the best spot for her student employees, said in reply to Hank's complaint: "I think Lizzie is trying hard to fit in. This is her first time working in food service, according to her file. If you're not happy with her work, it's up to you, Hank, to show her how to make the coffee properly."

"The coffee is excellent," Hank admitted. "Nobody can pull the combinations out of that machine like Lizzie. The other day, she got it to serve a Banana Split Chai Latte."

"But isn't that a good thing?" said Iris, sounding a little puzzled. "I thought the students liked ordering custom drinks."

"Oh, they do," admitted Hank. "And there's at least one fraternity running a bet on who can stump her. So far nobody has won."

"Then what is the problem?"

"Have you seen how she makes the drinks?" he said, sounding frantic to Lizzie. Of course, her view of Hank's waving arms, as well as his agitated complaints, were relayed by the tiny camera she'd left on the coffee machine so she could keep an eye on the register when she wasn't working. She felt some qualms about spying on her boss, but she'd promised Miss Gunderson she would look into the recent thefts in the Student Union. Small amounts had been disappearing from various registers. The thief always took only dollar bills in small denominations. Nobody could figure out how the thief did it. The camera was there for that. All the workers had been informed about the camera. If Hank had forgotten she could see and hear through it, that was his problem, she decided.

"What's wrong with how Lizzie is running the coffee machine?" asked Miss Gunderson.

"She doesn't touch it!" Hank flapped his hand at the automatic espresso machine. "She just lines up the cups, glances at it, and then the drinks start pouring out."

Miss Gunderson shook her head. "Still not sure what the problem is. I thought we put in these machines because the shot pour was automatic. Little training required, standardization of quality, and quick service. Push the button and achieve the perfect espresso drink."

"I know!" said Hank. "I went to that training seminar for these machines this summer. They were very clear that customizing espresso shots on the fly wasn't possible. But Lizzie does it. Without touching any button at all!"

Miss Gunderson sighed. "Now, Hank, we've talked about Cobalt City University. Some of our students, especially our local students, have certain skills. We want to honor that. Not everyone has to push the button the same way."

"But she doesn't push anything—" muttered Hank as he turned away. "She just looks at it. Sometimes she doesn't even do that. And where is she getting banana flavoring for the chai? We don't stock banana flavoring."

Later that day, Miss Gunderson and Lizzie discussed how to make Hank a little less stressed. At least that was how Miss Gunderson put it. Lizzie would have called it "to stop him from having the vapors again." But she understood that "hysteria" and "vapors" were words that had fallen out of favor in the last century. Time shifting was never easy. At least that's what her friend Tidwell said, and he'd lived enough centuries to see several languages change and the meaning of so many words go from deadly to friendly to forgotten. "Some words, thank all the household gods, are not used anymore," he said, "which improves the language immensely."

Lizzie agreed. Nothing was perfect in this particular year. But she'd seen worse. Smelled it too. That was the one thing she always noticed walking across the campus. The stench of coal smoke, horse dung, and rotten garbage wafting up from open sewers was a thing of the past, her past, and she didn't regret the disappearance of those odors.

She certainly welcomed the sight of thousands of women strolling around the campus, taking classes, teaching classes, and working in all parts of the University. All those women, assuming they could receive an education, forge a career, and lead the way for others. It definitely wasn't perfect. Lizzie was still flabbergasted by the fact that American politicians were still predominantly men. She had assumed when women won the vote, they would have used their power to at least balance out the halls of government on all levels. Still, she often thought, if only The Lady Detective or The Steel Suffragette had lived to see how much had changed. They would have been astounded to meet Miss Gunderson, in charge of so many employees, and so proud of her too.

So when Miss Gunderson asked Lizzie if she had any ideas to help Hank out, Lizzie suggested shifting to a library job for Saturday mornings, and rearranging her remaining schedule at the coffee stand so she was there when Hank was in class or at home.

"That's kind of you," said Miss Gunderson. "But Hank must learn to handle differences. I'm not sure if this is the best solution. I'd rather figure out a way to have you work together."

"Hank suffered that encounter with the worms," Lizzie reminded her. "I think it's that, more than me, but he probably would do better without any reminders."

"Oh yes," Miss Gunderson said. "I'd forgotten about that."

The worms arrived on campus from another dimension, a common problem in Cobalt City. Lizzie and her friends fought the wrigglers through the tunnels under the University. The wily other-dimensional creatures flowed up through the manhole covers to engulf a number of students. Luckily nobody was seriously hurt, but several, including Hank, still tended to flinch when they encountered an earthworm on a sidewalk after the rain.

"I could work the last shift on Sunday through Thursday nights," said Lizzie. "That's when Mark manages the stand."

"Oh, would you?" said Miss Gunderson. "He's such a sweet boy. I don't know why people don't want to be on the late-night shift with him."

Mark Obiyashi usually took the 10 p.m. to 2 a.m. shifts, the ones that closed the stand for the night. The issue for his co-workers and customers was that by midnight, the ghosts tended to gather. Mark did his best to discourage them, but his grandfather was a persistent spook. The old ghost had a tendency to rattle the little plastic spoons and other items on the self-help table when he was feeling particularly lonely. Lizzie knew Mark's grandfather found her own energy a bit disturbing—apparently he once told his grandson she gave him the "prickles" whenever she was nearby. If she was there, the ghost tended to behave. Besides, her "contestants" would follow her to a new time slot. The "Stump Lizzie" coffee movement ran its own social media feed, with people posting pictures of Lizzie's drink concoctions.

So Lizzie assured Miss Gunderson. ""I don't mind those hours, especially if it will give me Saturday mornings at the library. I've known Mark since my first year. We have many friends in common."

Mark sometimes yearned after Gizi, who used to live in the same dorm as Lizzie. This year, Lizzie had moved back to the Adventurers Club. As much as she liked all her new friends at the University, there were times when she just didn't want to pick her way through all the challenges that came with being a century or more older than everyone around her. It wasn't just missing more than a hundred years of history—she was also woefully behind on this generation's popular entertainment. At least when she was at the Club, streaming some movie with Tidwell, nobody said, "I can't believe you've never seen this."

The song changed on her playlist. The music was now slower and sadder. Lizzie rounded the corner of the aisle. A student was hunched in a study carrel, wedged into the window nook. The ivy outside crisscrossed the glass, casting shifting shadows on the carrel. Or perhaps the shadows entered the library with the young man sitting there. Recognizing the purple hoodie and ripped black jeans outfit, Lizzie called out, "Hello, Mark."

As always, it took Mark Obiyashi a minute to turn his head and acknowledge Lizzie with a half-hearted wave of his hand. "Hey," he said in his soft voice.

Lizzie smiled broadly. At least he'd heard her on the first try. There were so many voices trying to claim Mark's attention, he often missed simple greetings. Lizzie understood the problem. She had spent more than a century learning how to control, filter, and even ignore the distractions. The music in her ears faded away as she approached Mark. For the moment, she was intent on being present in one physical place rather than splashed across all of Cobalt City's electric networks.

"What are you doing here?" she asked Mark.

"Assignment," he pointed at the pile on the carrel's desk. A laptop, a couple of small notebooks, a multitude of pens, a blinking phone, and a crumpled print-out of a class assignment were piled next to his canvas messenger bag. Mark probably had upended it on the desk to find what he wanted. She'd seen him do that before. Parked under the desk was his beloved skateboard with its multiple ghost stickers.

"You've got a message," Lizzie said, nodding at the phone flashing in the center of the pile.

"Gizi," responded Mark, withdrawing even further into his hoodie. Lizzie could only see the tip of his nose and the edge of his chin. "Sending emojis."

"That's good?" Lizzie said. Their friend Gizi loved the language of pictures, and she combined the colorful little icons in creative ways. Figuring out what she meant ... that could be a challenge at times.

"It's a heart on fire," said Mark.

"Passionate love?" Lizzie responded.

"Or burning a past love and moving on," Mark answered. "We were texting about our favorite boba tea."

"New favorite drink?" said Lizzie, settling into this game of guessing what Gizi meant.

"Or she's over me," Mark slumped more. "Because I like tiger milk."

"What's Gizi's favorite?"

"Lychee snow. She's a wild girl," Mark said. He eyed his phone. "I guess I should send something back. Or I could work on this assignment." He poked at the paper crumpled on the desk.

"What are you working on?" Lizzie asked.

"I need to write about dragons." Mark heaved the sigh of the student taxed with a dull assignment, although Lizzie thought dragons sounded better than many of the subjects Mark regularly researched. "How different cultures see the dragons differently. It's an anthropology thing. I'm supposed to present something about the Nordic dragons, and my partner will respond with the Asian dragons." Then, in a tone of ultimate gloom, he added, "We have to give our research to the class using a slide deck."

Lizzie shuddered. She adored the power of computers, enjoyed access to many streaming services, and couldn't imagine ever living again without a phone in her pocket. But this century's insistence on placing bits of information on slides and forcing all the eyeballs in a room or in an online gathering to focus on those slides—that was a barbaric development. The only thing worse was being asked to create one of those instruments of tedious torture. It was the only part of being a combined history and communications student that she loathed.

"So who's your partner on this?" she asked Mark.

"Hello," said a deep voice behind Lizzie. She spun around to see a tall young man dressed in sharp contrast to Mark. If a white t-shirt could be said to be crisp, then this one was the ultimate in crispness, tucked with precision into dark blue jeans with knife-edge creases running from knee to ankle. The whole outfit, from top to bottom, appeared to be molded to the broad shoulders, muscled chest, narrow waist, and long legs of the young man facing her. Gizi would have responded with a heart bursting into flame, thought Lizzie. As it was, she fought to keep from flushing as he smiled at her.

"Oh, hey, Chao," said Mark, "this is Lizzie. We ... uh ... work together."

"Konglong Chao," said Mark's study partner. He reached out a warm, dry hand and shook Lizzie's hand with a formality that startled her. She'd grown used to waves, elbow bumps, hugs across her shoulders, and other casual greetings since returning to Cobalt City. This gesture felt like something from her past.

"Are you a student here too?" Chao asked. "I thought college students were older in the United States."

Lizzie knew her small size made her appear very young to many people. As did the fact that she'd been essentially frozen at 17 for so many long years in a virtual space beyond the physical realm. Others thought she would start aging now that she was a part of the physical world again. But Lizzie herself wasn't sure. She still felt the same as the day she was transformed into electricity by Steambolt Edison.

"I'm a student," she assured Chao. "Almost done with my degree too. Communications and history. At least that's my undergrad. I'm thinking about staying and going for a master's in library science." With the help of unlimited wealth from the Wrecker of Engines, Lizzie didn't need to worry about student loans. The timeless quality of a university life appealed to the young woman jolted out of her century. There were more than a few Cobalt City superheroes who used the alter ego of a harmless perpetual student to hide their true identity.

"An interesting combination of scholarly pursuits for a young woman," Chao replied. Mark had withdrawn more deeply into his carrel, poking at his phone and muttering at each emoji or gif he brought up. "Perhaps not as useful as others."

Lizzie drew a deep breath and recited all of Miss Gunderson's maxims about tolerance in the face of Chao's dismissive tone about her studies. Perhaps he thought she should be a math major. "And what's your major?" she asked.

"Myself, I am studying wealth," Chao said to Lizzie. "How to turn the power of money into an even grander supremacy of influence."

"Business major?" she asked. The flames inside died even more. She was sure someday, she would meet a business major who loved books and didn't spend all their time talking about their plans for an internship at one of Cobalt City's international banks. She just hadn't met that individual yet. On the other hand, most business majors were uncommonly good at making slide decks, so perhaps this was the right study partner for Mark.

"I am not a business major," Chao said, reviving Lizzie's interest. "Perhaps in time. But I am beginning with anthropology. I believe it is important to understand what makes humans ... ah ... human. Once that is understood, then matters can be better arranged."

He strolled to another study carrel. Unlike Mark's pile, Chao's computer, notebook, single pen, and slim leather briefcase were all lined up in a precise diamond shape. "North, south, east, west," Chao tapped each item once as he leaned over his desk. Looking over his shoulder, Lizzie noticed the center of the diamond was filled with small paper dragons.

"Oh, those are charming," she said. "Did you cut those?"

Each tiny dragon was cut from colored paper. Predominantly green colored paper, although some were brown, blue, yellow, or red.

Chao inclined his head. "Yes. It is an interesting art form. To balance both positive and negative space, turning an everyday object of insignificant value and available in multitudes into a creature exclusively its own being." He handed her one of the green-and-white dragons.

Lizzie balanced the tiny dragon on her palm. It was completely flat, not three dimensional like the origami creations some of her friends made. The green-and-white pattern printed on the dragon seemed familiar, but she was more intrigued by the shape created by Chao's art. The miniscule cuts in the paper delicately outlined the head, horns, and whiskers on one end, four legs ending in sharp talons, and a spiraling snake-like body that concluded with a tufted tail.

"The nine aspects of my paper dragon," said Chao, his finger hovering over her hand as he outlined his tiny creation from snout to tail. "From head to shoulder, from shoulder to breast, from breast to tail, the antlers of a stag, the head of a camel, the ears of the ox, the eyes of a demon, the teeth of a carp, the neck of a snake, the belly of a turtle, the claws of an eagle, and the tail of a tiger."

Even as he spoke, Lizzie felt a warm glow grow in her palm, a heat not unlike when she gathered energy to herself. But this didn't spark or sizzle like her own power. Instead, something nipped her hand with a sharp sting.

"Ow," Lizzie said. A minute line of blood trailed across the tip of her thumb. She carefully tipped the fragile paper dragon into her other hand. She sucked on her thumb to stop the bleeding. "A paper cut," she said. "How did I do that? I hate when that happens." She groped in her vest pocket, trying to fish out a tissue. "I don't want to bleed on your creature. Or any of the books!" She extended her other hand to Chao, intent on giving him back the tiny dragon.

"Fascinating," said Chao, looking down at the little green-and-white dragon that wobbled in the slight breeze caused by the movement of Lizzie's hand. "I thought only the demonic power of the ghost child could give them extra life. But you also seem to possess an abundance of energy, enough to spark at least a flight of dragons."

Lizzie blinked as the green dragon in her hand floated up in the air, suspended between herself and Chao. As the dragon flew in a slow loop-the-loop, she glimpsed a familiar eye floating in the center of a glowing triangle on its side. Suddenly she realized what the green-and-white markings of the dragon were.

"That's a one-dollar bill." As the dragon flew higher into the air, she added, "Or it used to be."

Chao looked pleased. "My first attempts to harness the energy of this world into my dragons came through the magical potency given by humans to this worthless paper. I favored the most powerful denomination to lend it extra demonic force. I heard on your newscasts the daily discussion of the worth of the American dollar in comparison to others. In classes too, I often heard the professors speak of the might of the American dollar and its influence for good and evil."

Lizzie backed away from Chao. "I don't think that's exactly what they meant. The power isn't actually in the money."

"No," said Chao, advancing on her. "I realized that when my little creatures failed to flourish. Simply making them out of money gave them the briefest spark of life. But then I found the remarkable Ghost House in Mark Obiyashi."

Mark, who was muttering at his phone, poked his head around the side of his study carrel at the sound of his name. "Oh, hey, Chao, sorry, I'll boot up my computer and get my information into our slides. Lizzie, how would you respond to a phone with an arrow emoji? Does Gizi want me to call her?"

"Mark!" said Lizzie, backing away from the dozens of tiny paper dragons rising out of Chao's study carrel. "Mark! We should leave now."

"What?" He stood up, looking past the desks to his study partner. "What's happening?"

A swarm of paper dragons now flew around Chao's head and shoulders. He pointed his hand towards Lizzie and Mark, like a man casting a ball or a spell at them. Where he pointed, the paper dragons flew. The green-and-white dollar dragons were particularly aggressive, darting forward to nip at Lizzie, but also easily distracted into fights with other dragons. Lizzie thought she saw a pair of dollar dragons attack a larger Euro banknote dragon. A sprightly *renminbi* dragon zipped under the trio to fly at Mark.

"Lizzie?" said Mark, swatting the Chinese people's money dragon away from his face. He swore as it bit at his wrist, trying for the veins there. "Ow! Stop that." He grabbed the determined dragon with his other hand, crumpling it into a small ball of paper, and throwing it away. "Lizzie, what are these things?"

"Run!" she responded, grabbing his hand, and pulling him into the stacks. The paper dragons flew after them.

Mark tugged back. "Wait," he said, lunging for his messenger bag and skateboard. "I'm not leaving these to get stolen."

"Run," Lizzie repeated, grabbing a book off a nearby shelf to swat away a few more dollar dragons.

Chao growled something between language and an animal's cry. He snatched his slender briefcase off the carrel desk and opened it. Another swarm of tiny currency dragons flew out of the case, coming straight at Mark and Lizzie.

Lizzie hooked one hand in Mark's collar and pulled him after her. Mark hopped on his skateboard and zipped around a corner. From old practice and countless fights with other villains, Lizzie swung herself up and around Mark to tandem ride his board. She locked her hands into his belt loops to hold herself on.

"What's attacking us?" Mark asked as they barreled around the corner and down the central hallway of the library.

"Money!" hissed Lizzie into Mark's ear. "Why did you pick him for a partner?"

"I didn't pick him. Chao picked me," said Mark, dodging as a Canadian dollar dragon swooped ahead of the rest and then dive bombed them like an angry Yukon mosquito. "And he said he was studying anthropology. The history of mankind's—"

Lizzie gave him a glare.

"The history of humanity," Mark corrected himself as they spun around another corner. "Our use of money to move ... oh damn." They reached the end of the bookcases and reached the graduate reading room. Long oak tables were centered in the middle of a faux Gothic hall. Green glass shaded lamps were set on top of the tables at intervals of a few feet. It was here that students could examine materials brought up from the archives, under the watchful eye of a librarian stationed at the end of the hall.

Lizzie and Mark simultaneously rolled off the skateboard and slid under a long group study table. Luckily, being Saturday morning, this particular section of the library was empty of students. As long as they stayed in the humanities, Lizzie knew, there was little chance of running into innocent bystanders. While there might be some math and science types in another section of the library, no self-respecting literature student was going to appear before noon on a weekend. In fact, most students wouldn't make it to the library until the last possible moment on Sunday night. Too many parties and D&D gatherings on Friday and Saturday nights, she knew.

"What was Chao studying?" Lizzie asked as they slithered under the table, swatting at the more aggressive dollar dragons that flew down to the floor. The bulk of the flock, for want of a better word, seemed to be content to fly up to the ceiling and spiral in the warm drafts created by the library's antiquated heating system.

"How money transfers power from one person to the next," said Mark. "He was a bit obsessed with it. Also cutting out those dragons. He kept doing that in the back of the classroom during all the lectures last week."

"Did you think that was odd?" said Lizzie.

"Nah," said Mark, "there's at least two women crocheting in the front of the room, another crafting chainmail at her desk, and then there's the guy who keeps making these creepy dolls."

"Creepy dolls guy?" she said.

"Yeah, I was keeping an eye on him," admitted Mark. "Dolls can go wrong in so many ways."

More paper dragons flew into the room, filling the space between their hiding spot and the door where they had just entered. Luckily the tiny beasts seemed fairly mindless away from Chao. Two Japanese yen dragons turned on a fluttering Peruvian Nuevo Sol. The latter sank beneath their superior fighting powers.

"Seriously, why did you pick Chao?" said Lizzie.

"Because he liked to do slide presentations," said Mark. "He said so."

"And that didn't tell you he was evil?" said Lizzie.

"It was either Chao or the creepy doll guy," said Mark. "Besides he just transferred into the class. Chao told me this was his first time in Cobalt City. I was trying to be nice to the new guy."

"That's the price of being a hero," Lizzie admitted. Then a dollar dragon spotted them and dived under the table. The nasty little creature got off a few nips and shreds of its paper claws before they managed to crush it beneath Mark's messenger bag.

Lizzie and Mark crawled the far end of the study table. Lizzie eyed an empty expanse of the marble floor that formed the lobby. There was a librarian's desk to one side of the massive oak doors, but whoever was supposed to be there must have left. Probably fetching a reference from the basement. Or confiscated Kit Kats from the breakroom.

"We should stop the dragons here," she said. "Before they escape into the quad."

"Yeah," said Mark, fussing with his skateboard. "Better than having another worm incident. Oh, did you know worm is another word for dragon in some cultures?"

"Yes," said Lizzie. She poked her head out from under the table to locate the flying swarm of dragons.

"Do you think everything we're learning in college is useless?" Mark said.

"Not everything," Lizzie said, ducking back under cover.

Mark rolled over on his back, flat on his board, his head pointed to the opening at the end of the table.

"Tell me when you want a push."

He grunted. As Lizzie watched, Mark's face began to blur and distend, as he became the superhero Ghost House. He looked at her with darkened eyes that reflected the void with tiny sparks of electric blue in their depths. Milky ectoplasm coiled off him like oily smoke. His clothes twitched and rippled as if being plucked by invisible hands. "Ready," said Mark in a voice that held the echoes of whispers beyond the veil.

Used to his transformation, Lizzie did not flinch. But an involuntary shudder shook her body as she laid hands on Mark's legs. Close contact translated to her senses as a feeling of frost or the chill she would receive by walking near the freezer section of the supermarket. She tried not to think about dead meat.

Gizi once told her that Mark's kisses felt as warm as anyone's. But Gizi probably never kissed him when he looked like this.

"Go!" said Mark, now fully transformed into the superhero Ghost House.

Lizzie shoved, giving the skateboard just an extra flash of her own power, so Mark shot into the center of the lobby in a shower of sparks arcing off the metal axles. A few of the bolder dragons, diving at Mark, caught fire or were crushed under his skateboard wheels. Others became entangled in the nets of ectoplasmic energy he wove around them. Mark flipped up and landed feet first on his skateboard's tail. With the tail of the board on the marble floor, he ran up the rest and into the air, spreading his arms wide as he threw off blast after blast of ghostly energy.

Lizzie rolled to the side and sprang from under the table just behind the flock of paper dragons intent on swarming Mark. From the corner of her eye, she saw her own reflection in the long windows lining the reading hall. She was completely manifesting the Electric Girl, her clothing now transformed to her white shirtwaist, long tweed coat, and divided skirt. This was the uniform of her days as the intrepid girl reporter of nineteenth-century Cobalt City. Her hair coiled off her shoulders into the practical braided bun of her past, and her beloved "newsies" cap appeared atop her head. The feather that had once decorated her hat was now as bright as flame, glowing white with the heat of her power.

Lizzie plunged her hands into the swarm of dragons, intent on overwhelming them with jolts of pure electricity. The little creatures clawed and bit, but Lizzie now bled sparks that set their fragile bodies aflame. Little wisps of ash drifted to the floor.

"No!" A roar shook the room.

Lizzie spun around and saw Chao enter the hall. With one smooth leap, he vaulted to the top of the oak reading table and ran down its length. As he ran, he transformed, his body elongating like a snake, his hands outstretched like "the claws of an eagle," Lizzie breathed. And, yes, his nose now appeared very camel-like as the stag horns sprouted from his head.

Chao launched himself directly at Mark. But Lizzie manifested her own wings, shooting like a shower of fireworks from her shoulders, cyan feathers burning with the power of the city. She launched herself at Chao, knocking him away from Mark with a sizzle of electric power.

They rolled across the marble floor, banging against the solid oak furniture and then twisting up to the vaulted ceiling to race across the wooden beams and down again into the diminishing flock of dragons. As Chao swooped and twisted, biting and clawing at Lizzie, she continued to counterpunch. Concentrating on stunning rather than harming, she was hampered by Chao's manifestation of his scales. One blow to his stomach rang off a belly as hard as a turtle. She spun away, shaking her hand and wondering if she had broken any bones.

Chao opened his mouth and roared again, loud enough to rattle the library's windows in their frames. He sprang for Lizzie.

With a push of her electric wings, Lizzie flew over Chao's head and then twisted in mid-air. She reached down with one burning hand and latched onto his bull's ear.

Chao yelled in pain. Lizzie twisted harder, forcing him down to the floor. As he subsided, the last of the paper dragons collapsed in Mark's ectoplasm net.

"I yield! Yield!" Chao said. He was now almost human, all but the twitching ear that Lizzie still pinched in her burning fingers. Shedding his ghostly aspect, Mark walked up to them. "Not cool," he said to Chao, "feeding your study partner to your paper currency dragons."

Chao bowed his head even further. "I beg your humble pardon," he said. "I only meant to find a way to bring greater order to humanity."

Lizzie let her wings fold back into her being. She lifted her hand from Chao's ear, which transformed from its furry bovine shape to a more human look.

"Various people have tried that throughout history," she said. "Imposing order, especially supernatural or super powered order, never ends well."

"But this world is so messy," Chao complained as he sat up. "It needs order." He rolled away from them. "And the King in Yellow commands!" With a shout, he pulled a leather wallet from his back pocket. He opened it to release another small batch of dollar dragons. "Kill!" he cried, pointing at Lizzie and Mark.

"Now really," said a voice from the far end of the hall. "What are you kids doing?" It was the Saturday morning librarian, almost obscured by a huge stack of books in her arms. She thumped the reference books down on her desk.

Distracted by the returning librarian, Chao glanced away. Lizzie let loose the lightning bolt she'd been restraining between her two hands. It arced through the air, attracted to Chao like he was a giant lightning rod. As the energy passed through the dragon, he burst into smoke and ash. For a moment, Lizzie glimpsed a world behind him, a swirling cosmos of chaos that reminded her of her own electrical prison past.

Then with a sizzle, the dragon and his paper children were gone.

The librarian glanced up from her desk. "What was that?" she said. "Are those lights shorting again? The janitor was supposed to fix that."

"Just a light bulb popping," said Lizzie as Mark grabbed his skateboard and his messenger bag from the floor. He stomped with relish one weakly wiggling dollar dragon.

"Those lights need to be replaced someday," said the librarian turning back to her books. "Oh, did you need help finding something?"

"No, no, we're done here," said Lizzie, pulling Mark toward the outer door.

The librarian gave a look of disapproval at Mark's skateboard. "No using that in here," she said.

"Of course not," said Mark as if he hadn't already zipped through several reference sections on his wheels.

Other than a few small piles of ash from disintegrated dragons, the hall looked much as it had before their fight. Cobalt City had learned to build strong, to withstand the clash of titans within its borders.

"Everyone complains about money," said Lizzie to Mark as they left the library. "I guess I understand why Chao thought it would be a good thing to use in his spell. Money is an evil force, and all that."

"Necessary evil," said Mark. "Hard to go back to a barter only system. But order just makes everyone miserable. And anarchy doesn't work either. Everything to the strong and nothing to the weak. He obviously didn't listen to any of the lectures."

Lizzie shrugged. "His loss. That's what college is for. To debate these things. To learn."

Mark's phone beeped again. "Gizi?" asked Lizzie.

"Yep," said Mark. "I know this one." He flashed her an emoji of a hungry face surrounded by a fork and knife. "She wants a snack break."

"Tell her to come to the coffee stand," said Lizzie. "I'll make her something special to go with the muffin."

"Won't Hank be there?" said Mark as they walked across the campus.

"Yes," said Lizzie with a twinkle. "Time to open up his mind a little. I think I will make a double banana chai latte with whipped cream and a cherry on top."

"Does the machine do that?" said Mark.

"It will after I get through with it," said Lizzie.

Rosemary Jones has been writing in the Cobalt City universe since the first Christmas anthology. She enjoys hanging out with superheroes as much as she can. Her other published fiction includes two novels set in the Forgotten Realms: *City of the Dead* and *Crypt of the Moaning Diamond.* Currently she's writing about eldritch troubles in the 1920s for the Arkham Horror series published by Aconyte, including *Mask of Silver* (2021). You can find her at twitter.com/rosemaryjones chattering about books, games, arts events, and, occasionally, hedgehog trivia.

Mother of Harlots

by Erik Scott de Bie

And there followed another angel, saying, Babylon is fallen, is fallen, that great city, because she made all nations drink of the wine of the wrath of her fornication.
~ Revelation 14:8, the Holy Bible, King James Version

When the three teenage girls swept through the doors of Cain's Dive, dripping from the haze of rain that had been falling all day, Vivienne knew they would be trouble.

Worse, because the ringleader of this little clique? The sixteen-year-old pulling back her hood to shake out her long blonde curls like something out of a Teen Vogue photoshoot? Hair that seemed just discordant enough with her Latina features to be striking and memorable? The sort of look that had already attracted the attention of more than one fashion magazine, which the girl had babbled about to her *ad nauseum*, i.e., until Vivienne had to excuse herself to go use the bathroom and never returned?

That was Angel Desantes, also known as the superhero A-Girl. Striding into her bar like she owned the place. With two minions in tow.

"Uh oh," Andre said, looking up from wiping glasses behind the bar. "That looks like trouble."

"Yeah."

Vivienne had meant to put the Jack Daniels back on the shelf. Instead, she found herself pouring a triple. She nodded toward the table where the girls were making themselves comfortable. Looked like they were here to stay. Which probably meant they'd want to be served.

"Business is business," Andre said.

"Maybe just card them and tell them to get the fuck out?" she asked, daring to hope.

"Minors can sit in the front, V."

"Look, whose bar is it?"

"I'm just reading the sign." Andre pointed past her at the sign that listed the day's specials, the Wi-Fi password, and—sure enough—where customers under twenty-one could be served. Specifically, the front room.

"Well, shit." Vivienne sighed. "Odds or evens?"

"Odds."

They tapped their fists together three times and extended fingers: Andre two, Vivienne three.

"Fuck," she said.

"One of these days, maybe you'll even win that game."

Vivienne's three extended fingers became one.

Andre grinned. "I'll fire up the grill."

Vivienne, defeated more soundly than that one time against the Cold Equalizer in Venezuela, grabbed a notepad and skulked toward the front of the bar. Cain's Dive was her turf—her safe place, her sanctum—and she wasn't a fan of reality intruding. But because it was her territory, she knew it better than anyone. She knew, for instance, about the odd corner around the wall where she could stand between the bar and the front of the Dive, where she could stand and only customers at one of the tables would see her. The table at which the girls sat was not that table. There she lurked for a second, listening to size them up a bit, where she could just peek out and see what she was walking into.

That and use her powers, which never quite quieted down for anything short of a blackout drunk, and even she couldn't get that going at 3:30 in the afternoon. Ugh, it wasn't even happy hour yet.

"I didn't know we were coming to a bar," said the dark-haired girl of the trio. "Are we allowed to be in here?"

"Is that him?" asked Angel's other friend—a redhead.

"Who, that tall black guy behind the bar?" asked the first girl, a smile curling her delicate features. Vivienne pegged her as Japanese heritage-wise, but the way she spoke was entirely American. Second- or third-generation, at least. She seemed a little familiar, like maybe Vivienne had seen her before. "He is pretty hot, I'm not gonna lie."

44

"Why's it gotta be about his race?" Angel asked, which momentarily stunned the others, until Angel grinned. "Jeez, Yumi! You're so easy."

"Hey!" the dark-haired girl protested. "I am *not*."

"That's not what Josh Tramm says," the other girl said.

Angel busted up laughing and promptly slammed her knee into the table, knocking over the salt and pepper shakers. Clumsy as always.

The redhead had long red hair and light blue eyes, and Vivienne pegged her as younger than both of the others: softer spoken but sharp. She picked her moment. Not a lot of emotion coming off her—she was carefully controlled, but Vivienne thought there was something underneath ...

"Ouch, Claire," Yumi said with a grin. "Brutal."

"Andre *is* pretty hot, but you're not his type, Yumi," Angel said, chiming in.

Yumi smirked. "What, Asians?"

"Yeah, that's *definitely* what I meant."

That just left Angel herself. Vivienne didn't like feeling a superhero's emotions on a good day, and even less so this particular heroine's vibes. Angel was in a good mood, full of that peppy spirit that would have driven Vivienne to drink if she weren't already a moderately functioning alcoholic. Ugh. Kids.

"Oh hey, it's you, A." Yumi pointed up at the front room TV, which had just then chosen to show Angel prancing around in some kind of skimpy schoolgirl getup—technically within the bounds of taste, if not propriety—and singing, though the Dive kept the TVs on mute with closed captioning. The song probably would have made Vivienne's head ache worse. "You look great there."

"Oh, stop," Angel said, and mostly meant it. Praise always seemed to make her anxious.

"You didn't answer my question," Claire said. "Is that the bartender you were telling us about? You know, the one you keep—?"

She trailed off, as Yumi had locked eyes on Vivienne, and her face took on a hard-to-read expression—something a bit like embarrassment mixed with excitement. Vivienne knew that look, as well as the accompanying hit of fluttery emotion. The rush was so powerful it overwhelmed the alcohol's best efforts to dampen her powers.

Girl had a crush. Adorable.

"Afternoon," Vivienne said, which was the most approachable she could manage.

At the sound of her voice, Angel turned with a wide smile. "Oh hey," she said. "These are my friends, Yumi Kujikawa and Claire Anderson. Friends, this is my Aunt V."

"Wait, *aunt?*" Yumi's face lost all color. "She's your *aunt?*"

"Unfortunately," Vivienne said, to a chorus of confused looks. "Funny story, actually. I told my sister, 'oh no, Athena, kids ruin your life, and the last person you want to make one with is Antonio 'Fascist Fuckboy' Desantes, but what are you gonna do." She managed to avoid saying a certain part of the anatomy wants what it wants, which she took as a sign of growth. Instead, she flipped open the notebook. "What can I get you ladies?"

Yumi had gone red as a teacher's apple, while Claire just looked confused, like she was trying to solve an unexpected math problem on the specials board.

Angel rolled her eyes. "Pay no attention to my cringey aunt," she said. "She was never house trained."

"Hey, you're in *my* house," Vivienne said. "We do a different kind of training here."

"Okay, boomer," Angel said.

"Hey, I'm Gen X," Vivienne said. "Not that you'd remember."

"Gen *XXX*, maybe."

"Ooh, witty."

Yumi gave a little "meep" sound, as though that last extremely bad quip finally broke her. "You, uh—"

"What are your salads?" Claire asked, with the sort of smile one reserves for hospitality workers.

Vivienne turned to her, finally in professional mode. "Cobb, Caesar, spinach-walnut," she said.

"Spinach, I guess." Claire pursed her lips. "And what's in the house vinaigrette?"

"It's vinegar and olive oil," Vivienne said. "With mustard."

"Stone ground?"

"Dijon."

Claire looked mildly disappointed, but she nodded anyway.

"Irish nachos, extra-large, tots instead of fries," Angel said. "Thanks, Aunt V."

"Uh huh." She looked to Yumi. "And what can I get you, princess?"

"Uh." Yumi looked desperately at the menu, flipping the pages back and forth without rhyme or reason, looking for an escape it just wasn't offering.

"She'll have the same," Angel suggested. "They're really good. Fries covered in cheese. Or get 'em with tots, like I do."

"What makes them Irish?" Claire asked.

"The scallions," Vivienne said. "Or, y'know, the beer cheese."

"Cheese?" Yumi asked. "Oh, uh, I'm lactose intolerant."

"Better get the Mediterranean plate, then," Vivienne said. "It's the best vegan thing on the menu."

"Oh, uh, okay," Yumi said, entirely incapable of meeting Vivienne's eye. She seemed extremely shy all of a sudden, fidgeting with her hands under the table.

"Anything to drink?" Vivienne asked, receiving essentially blank stares. "Waters all around?"

"The strawberry lemonade has free refills, right?" Angel asked.

Vivienne sighed. "Yes."

It was only when she walked away and passed behind the eavesdropping corner that she heard the tension break in a series of awkward giggles.

"Jesus," Yumi said. "You knew all about this, and you just let me go on and on—"

Angel laughed. "Oh my God, your *face*."

"What are you guys talking about?" Claire asked.

"Oh, nothing," Angel said. "Yumi's just embarrassed."

"Embarrassed?" Yumi asked. "Your aunt was responsible for my bisexual awakening. I am *mortified*."

"Your what?" Claire asked, blinking.

Vivienne felt something spike from Claire—a weird, unexpected feeling that made the world spin for a second, and left her dizzy. Wow, she wouldn't have thought something like that was even possible.

She headed back behind the bar, wobbling a little bit on her feet.

"Girl, how much did you *have*?" Andre asked.

"That's not ... whatever." She tore off the order and handed it over.

"I already started making the tots," Andre said. "She wants a double, right?"

"Better make it a triple. You know how much she eats."

Andre nodded sagely. They'd both personally watched Angel single-handedly eat an entire large Chicago-style pizza in one sitting. Angel took in at least 10,000 calories a day, and that assumed she didn't go flying around punching trucks through buildings. The more she used her powers, the hungrier she got.

"Are you all right?" Andre asked.

"Yeah, fine," Vivienne said. "Pour me a Full House, would you? Triple Jack, double Crown."

"Jesus, V," Andre said. "They're just girls, and they don't even look that mean."

"It's a powers thing." Vivienne rubbed her temples. "I'm just ... it's a lot. The one has a thing for me, and the other ... I don't even know."

That name "Kujikawa" sounded familiar, but she couldn't quite place it.

Andre looked concerned. "Do you need a break? I can bring them their food."

At first, Vivienne thought about refusing, but it made a lot of sense. Her stomach roiled, her head throbbed, and her bladder suddenly felt full. "Yeah, I've gotta pee."

She made her way to the bathroom, moving in drunken loops that became even more pronounced as she went. She hadn't felt like this since she'd downed a fifth of vodka in one sitting. So, since last night. It made it hard to think, let alone walk.

The mighty Vengeance, said the voice in her head. *Undone by a child.*

"Fuck off," she murmured under her breath.

The Dive had a single, unisex bathroom, set with a convenient bar for disabled customers that Vivienne had used on more occasions than she could count. She grasped Old Faithful firmly and let herself slip down onto the closed toilet seat. Cognitively, she knew she'd need to strip to do her business, but the dizziness overwhelmed her, and she thought just sitting there for a minute might be nice. Just a minute ...

~

When Vivienne started back to the world, the lights were off except for the green-glowing exit sign, and the room felt cold. Had she fallen asleep? Her neck protested any attempts to move, so that checked out. She'd definitely used the toilet at some point, for both ends. At least she still had her hair tied back, which she recalled Andre had suggested before she started drinking. That man was worth his weight in Johnnie Walker Blue.

She rubbed her aching head. "Fuck, Andre, you could have at least knocked. What if I choked on my own vomit or something?"

Probably shed a few tears, arrange a tasteful funeral, then inherit the business and run it a *lot* better.

She turned on the water to wash her hands. Had to appease the Health Department, after all. The tap sputtered and shot out a few disconsolate spurts of dirty water, then just groaned.

"Huh." Vivienne thought they were paid up on utilities. Maybe she was a worse boss than she thought.

The lights didn't come on either; she flipped the switch a couple times just to make sure.

"If you can keep the lights on, maybe you *should* be the boss, Andre."

And what was she *wearing*? Some kind of skimpy, bikini thing and lots of necklaces and bangles. What, was it Pride week? She hadn't been to one of those marches in years. At least her black leather jacket was still hanging on the wall, dimly illumined in the weird green light, and she slid that on.

Only then, when she opened the door, did the full scope of the situation make itself clear.

For a start, the bathroom door opened into little more than a burned-out husk of a hallway, the twisted, half-melted remnants of the interlaced metal framework curling like fingers toward her. The bar itself was gone, as were most of the buildings on the block. All around her, Seattle was an utter ruin, flames and smoke rising from the skeletons of destroyed apartment towers, gutted houses, and the collapsed supermarket down the street. Several vehicles, from which flames rose freely, hung over the edges of the shattered remains of a parking structure whose shopping complex had caved into the middle. In the distance to the south, she could barely make out the hulking ruins of skyscrapers amongst the smoke of the city proper.

Vivienne Cain had taken a nap, and the world had ended in the meantime. Typical.

What was it this time? Zombies? Nuclear war? Or maybe …

"Is this you, Azazel?" she asked aloud, but got no answer. The one time she wanted to hear from her abusive ex, he was silent.

Maybe that should have told her what she needed to know, but Vivienne Cain had never been too quick on the uptake. And she had a massive hangover anyway.

Vivienne found herself sprawling, thrown away on a massive shockwave, and the world shook and splintered all around her. She smashed flat on her butt and tumbled backward to land on her belly in the muddy puddle that used to be the parking lot behind the Dive.

"The f—?"

A flash of movement caught her eye, and instinct honed over years of combat training and practice sent her rolling out of the way as a massive, scaled appendage smashed down across the lot. Had she stayed put, it would have flattened her. She sat there, covered in mud and soot, and looked at the snake-like thing the size of a freight train and studded with spines as long and sharp as swords.

It was a tail.

She staggered up, heart thudding in her throat as the thing started to move, shuddering as muscles rippled below the scales. Ponderously, it began to lift off the ground, each chilling click of the spines stabbing into Vivienne's head with a little jolt of fear. Pointedly, it was her *own* fear, rather than anything she could absorb and redirect. She felt empty—hollowed out. And now she was about to die.

Another, much smaller figure landed next to her, strong hands went under her armpits, and Vivienne found herself hurtling away as the tail swept across the lot, tossing skeletons of cars aside like dust bunnies. Vivienne looked up, blinking, at the figure flying her away from the devastation, and wouldn't have recognized her without the pink energy trail.

"Angel?" she asked, having to shout over the wind whipping past her ears.

"I got you!" Angel—dressed in an honest-to-Hildegaard suit of shining metal armor, of all things—glanced down at her and nodded, her golden hair flowing wildly and trailing off into pink flames. "Yumi's got the dragon!"

Dragon?

Only then did Vivienne understand the scope of the monstrosity: a massive reptilian form, as big as a skyscraper, from which bristled half a dozen clawed hands and—she counted— seven heads, no two of them alike. Some of the creature's faces were long and tapered like those of wolves, while others bore the beaks of vicious raptors, and still others came to upturned, hog-like noses or terminated in the rounded jaw and glittering fangs of snakes. Each head, she saw, bore at least one sharp horn, and upon each horn sat a massive crown of gleaming black metal set with glittering crystal. She counted ten horns and ten crowns in total.

Well. *That* was some imagery.

The beast, that familiar voice in her head said. *Witness a beast that rises from the sea—it has seven heads, and upon those head, ten horns with ten crowns ...*

Vivienne was too afraid even to reply with a witty retort. She couldn't remember the last time she'd felt this kind of genuine terror—she didn't seem to feel fear the way other people did, not after so much experience with it. Over her life, she'd tasted and experienced the gamut of horrors, and very little shook her. She was definitely shaking now, however, and there was no way her niece hadn't noticed. Ugh. How embarrassing.

And somewhere, in the midst of all that, she felt one source of white-hot *rage.* Something out there was furious, and it wouldn't temper that anger until it had righteous satisfaction.

Speaking of which, the dragon raised one massive claw and, ponderously, moved it toward Angel and Vivienne as they flew. Its limb had several segments and moved slowly, as a creature of such scale, but considering the breadth of its impact area, that hardly seemed to matter.

"A?" Vivienne cried. "*A!*"

Finally, Angel looked over at the claw unspooling toward them, and Vivienne shuddered as they abruptly changed direction. Not only was Angel not too good at flying while carrying someone, as evidenced by Vivienne's stomach rising into her throat, but it all seemed moot; this seemed like trying to dodge a falling building.

That was when she saw the trail of flames burning down the creature's arm, from its shoulder toward one of its three elbows.

Vivienne could make out a slim feminine figure: one that wore a frilly dress and corset like something halfway between a D&D LARP and a Renaissance faire porn parody, and held what appeared to be a flaming sword. Even as the claw swept toward them, the sword-wielder swept the fiery weapon overhead, then plunged it into the creature's elbow with enough force to sink nearly to the hilt, so the flames all but vanished.

An ear-splitting roar filled the sky, and the claw flinched away to miss them narrowly—so narrowly that the wind of its passing buffeted them away like flies. The force broke Angel's grasp, and Vivienne tumbled end over end, the world spinning wildly. The ground rushed up to meet her, and she sucked in breath to scream or, more likely, swear.

Then arms wrapped around her, and Angel pulled Vivienne up into an arc down and through, missing the ground by a few feet, and finally dumped her unceremoniously atop the ruins of the Dive. Vivienne stumbled and nearly fell over the broken wall and was about to curse her niece out when she saw Angel land so hard it put a small crater in what was left of the roof. In retrospect, Vivienne was glad the girl had dropped her rather than tried to carry her through that landing.

"You all right?" Angel flipped up the visor of her helmet. "Aunt V?"

"Yeah," Vivienne said, despite her heart pounding in her head. She tried not to wheeze as she looked at the massive draconic ... *thing*. "What's going on?"

"Aw, man," Angel said. "I was hoping you'd know."

Vivienne searched for the girl who had struck the creature, and it took a second to make her out: half-sliding, half-running down the creature's tail toward them. As they approached, the figure leaped off the tail and landed on the creaking roof beside them, legs spread wide, one hand on the roof to keep balance. It was Angel's friend, Vivienne realized, in that campy medieval-esque dress and a curved sword in her hands, its hilt, handle, and pommel wrought in red leather, its scabbard red lacquer. In terms of emotions coming off her, Vivienne primarily felt excitement and a little trepidation—the emotional mode of a ruthless, highly skilled warrior.

"Nice one, Yumi!" Angel held up a hand.

"Yeah!" The girl stood up and high-fived Angel, then bounced around in a celebratory circle.

Vivienne raised one eyebrow. "What?"

"Oh, sorry!" Yumi Kujikawa smiled a goofy smile. "I got a little carried away." Then she flushed a little at Vivienne, and particularly her revealing outfit. "What, uh ... what are you wearing?"

"I just assumed it was one of her costumes," Angel said. "They're all like that."

Vivienne ignored the question. She'd finally made a connection. It was the sword. "Kujikawa," she said. "Of Kujikawa Industries? Related to Eiko, by any chance?"

Yumi blinked at her rapidly. "You ... you knew my mother?"

Small world. "The Silver Echo? Sure."

Now it was Angel's turn to look startled. "Who? What's she talking about, Y?"

"Um," Yumi said. "A, you know how I'm such a good fencer?"

"Yeah?" Angel's eyes widened. "Oh my God! Your mom's a cape, too!"

"Was," Vivienne corrected. "I was sorry to hear about the accident."

"Thanks." Yumi looked away.

"And that's Eiko's sword, I'm guessing."

"Uh, yeah," Yumi said.

That was good. It meant they had a chance.

Vivienne took that opportunity to look back up at the dragon. It was still mewling in pain but didn't seem to know where they had gone. That, or it was too busy doing ... whatever it was doing. Ushering in the end of the world, probably. So they had breathing room, but not much of it.

Tick tock, Vengeance, Azazel said in her head.

Yumi made a little sound, and Vivienne got a jolt of fear from the young woman. When she looked, Yumi had gone pale and put her hand on the handle of the Muramasa sword. Flames had begun to leak out around its hilt.

"What's wrong?" Angel took up a fighting stance. "Is something coming?"

"Nope," Vivienne said, not moving a muscle. "Your BFF has just put two and two together."

"What?"

Sure enough, Yumi had set her jaw. "If you're Angel's aunt, that means you—you're—"

"Yes," Vivienne said. "Trust me, kid. I'm the last one you should be afraid of. Well, second-to-last."

"Hey!" Angel said, then frowned. "Was that about me?"

Vivienne kept looking at Yumi. "Let's just get out of this, and then you can draw that thing if you still feel like you have to. But don't draw it now, because that's something you can't take back. Right?"

"You really do know my mother." Yumi eased her hand off the sword. "So, uh, what do we do?"

"Team up!" A ridiculous smile spread across Angel's face.

"First things first," Vivienne said. "We get somewhere safe. Get some food. Some real clothes." She picked at her extremely slutty getup. "Then we figure out what the hell is going on."

And from the looks of things, she meant that literally.

~

Whatever apocalyptic cataclysm had befallen Seattle the previous night, there were some things it couldn't change. The Raven's Rookery, i.e., the Supergroup safehouse in Sodo, was basically a fallout shelter, and would probably withstand the end of the world if it came to it. Fortunately, it still recognized Vivienne's voice and granted access—also, the sentry guns powered down, prompting a relieved sigh. She stretched, because her whole body hurt.

"What?" Angel asked. "You didn't think it would work?"

"I thought it might kill us," Vivienne said, rubbing her side where Angel had wrapped an arm around her. Her niece wasn't any better at carrying two people than one. "Your dad hasn't forgiven me for ripping out his eye."

"Oh right! Ha ha! You're so funny, Aunt V." Angel looked to Yumi. "You okay, Y?"

"Huh? Oh, uh, sure, A. I'm fine."

"Whew!" Angel declared. "Good to know! Go team!"

Yumi looked a little dizzy, or maybe sleepy. To Vivienne, though, who could feel the girl's emotions more clearly than her own, it seemed pretty obvious how she felt.

She felt that way too. Also, extremely tired.

54

They hadn't seen any people on the way down here—just a series of burned outlines into buildings, and the blackened remains of clothing on the street and in burning cars. Whatever happened, it had annihilated everyone in Seattle—everyone but them. A mass death event was a tough thing for a world-class veteran hero to take in, let alone a seventeen-year-old girl whose biggest worry was getting the right prom dress.

It was prom season, wasn't it? Vivienne couldn't keep up with these things.

Anyway, where Yumi became increasingly detached and Angel raced her own rising anxiety with increasingly over-the-top pep, Vivienne remained cool and in control. This wasn't, after all, her first apocalypse, and she had a feeling all wasn't as it seemed. That, and someone had to be the adult in the room, so she kept her own fears at bay.

That's what she told herself, anyway—not the more obvious answer, that she was a psychopath without normal, functioning emotions.

Occam likes his razors, my dear, said her ever-present companion.

In a way, she found it comforting. That Azazel was still talking to her meant she hadn't lost her mind.

The safehouse—she wouldn't say "rookery"—was exactly as Supergroup had left it, which made it perfect for lying low: rooms full of couches, refrigerators full of snacks, shelves upon shelves of canned food, and a few gadgets—mostly refills for traversal equipment a power-suited hero might use. And, because it was built by the Raven, it had several advanced labs and tech rooms that rejected Vivienne's access. Probably for the best—odds seemed good Vivienne would just end up blowing herself up if she tried to use any of that crap.

Angel, of course, loved it.

"I've never been in one of these!" she said. "I know my dad talked about 'em all the time, but dude! Whoa!" She trailed her fingers along the blue cape of one of the costumes on display in the ostentatiously wide hallway. "Are these real?"

"Yeah." Vivienne hit a switch, and the lights flicked on progressively down the hall, illumining a dozen such costumes on manikins. They ranged from the sensible and tactical to the outright cartoonish, but each one fairly barfed color. "The cape scene in Seattle always had a flair for the dramatic."

"Wow." Yumi looked around at the uniforms and settled on one on a femme mannikin: a getup comprising black silks with a few attendant spikes, bits of red, and twin scarlet capes that flowed from the back. "Is that Bloodmoon? Oh man, I remember my mom—" She shook her head. "So cool."

"Kind of ghoulish, if you ask me," Vivienne said. "They say serial killers keep trophies just like this."

That shut them both up. Angel's wide grin turned to something brittle and desperate, and Yumi smiled wanly. If they wanted to bask in the glow of bygone heroism, who did it hurt? It was good to see the girls focusing on something other than the existential dread of the end of the world.

"There should be some clothes if you want to change." Vivienne checked the structural integrity of her leather jacket, which was holding up pretty well. Dragon attack, road rash, no biggie. "And grab something to eat. A, there are high calorie MREs in the cabinet marked Justice. He had super metabolism too. I think they're like 2,000-calorie Pop Tarts."

"What's MRE stand for?" Angel asked.

"The fuck if I know," Vivienne said. "Made ready to eat, I guess."

"*Meal* ready to eat," Yumi said. "My, uh, brother is in the army." Her face took on a shadow. "*Was*, I guess."

"Hey," Angel said. "Don't think like that! Positive mental attitude. Aunt V can fix this. Right, Aunt V?"

By way of answer, Vivienne shrugged and broke the seal on a slightly dusty bottle of twelve-year Scotch.

She flopped down on the couch and rubbed her aching head. If she'd felt tired before, she felt positively drained now. Worn out, as though she'd spent the entire night before running a marathon, rather than drinking herself into oblivion. Come to think of it, had she really had that much?

"Hey, uh," Angel put a hand on Yumi's arm. "I didn't mean to make you upset."

"She's not upset," Vivienne said, gesturing with the bottle. "She's embarrassed."

Angel frowned. "Huh? Why?"

Yumi looked away and said nothing.

"Yay," Angel said. "I'll just, um, check that cabinet. Maybe they have strawberry flavor?" She left Yumi and Vivienne alone.

Yumi stepped over to the opposite couch and perched on the arm, looking nervous. Even so, she had a remarkable degree of composure to her—a sense of perfect balance that Vivienne had only seen in a few people before. Olympian levels of poise and coordination. And for being American born and raised, she certainly had an element of Japanese reserve to her. Definitely Eiko's daughter.

"Spit it out, kid," Vivienne said. "I'm not psychic, and I'm definitely not a shrink. Talk, so we can get past it."

When Yumi looked back up, her cheeks were bright red. "Sorry, it's just ... Lady Vengeance! Wow. And not only are you my friend's aunt, but you also knew my mother. And now I, uh—"

"And now you've got an age-inappropriate crush," Vivienne said. "It's no big deal. Welcome to the bisexual disaster lifestyle."

"Pansexual," Yumi said.

Vivienne shrugged. "That works."

"Straight." They both looked at Angel as she entered the room, pink powerlines gleaming against the black of the costume she wore. She shrugged. "I thought we were comparing orientations."

"I see you found the Mark 2 suit," Vivienne said. "Tony made that for you, you know, when you were old enough." Which at seventeen, she absolutely wasn't, but hey, you couldn't be choosy at the end of the world.

"It fits perfectly," Angel said. "It's stretchy."

"That's the nanofibers," Vivienne said. "It's probably bulletproof, too. Though, I mean—" She gestured to Angel with the bottle. "A for Ablative, maybe?"

"Oh shit," Yumi said. "We should go around and share our mantle, huh. If we're really going to team up!"

"Yeah!" Angel said. "That's practically in the handbook."

"Mantle?" Vivienne sighed. "You mean codenames. Are we really doing this?"

"A-Girl!" Angel said brightly. "A for Awesome! A for Amazing! A for Effort!" She rolled her eyes. "Parker said it tested well."

"Yeah, we know," Vivienne murmured, but only the scotch heard her. Both girls looked at her expectantly, and she rolled her eyes. "What is this, Heroes Anonymous?"

More like Villains Anonymous, Azazel whispered.

She didn't bother arguing, because he was right.

"Hi, I'm Lady Vengeance," she said, only able to say it because of the scotch.

It almost seemed like she should follow up her introduction with a list of her sins. *I'm an alcoholic. I'm an addict. I tore out Tony's eye once.* Not that she said those things, but they were all part of her "mantle"—inextricable from her story.

She could almost hear the chorus of greetings in her head. *Hi, Lady Vengeance.* Like a condemnation.

The girls seemed energized, not depressed. They would learn.

"I'm Muramasa," Yumi said with a bit less enthusiasm. "It's, uh, new. I haven't even gone out on patrol yet. I haven't even made a costume."

"Awesome," Angel said. "I mean, the name. Costumes are cool too."

Vivienne smirked behind the bottle. Says the girl who wears a glorified NASCAR tracksuit, complete with advertisements. At least the outfit she had on now wasn't that atrocity.

"Muramasa Sengo was a legendary swordsmith, right?" Vivienne pointed to Eiko's sword in its red scabbard. "He make that?"

"Yeah." Yumi ran her fingers reverently down the scabbard. "Our, uh, ancestral blade. It's cursed."

"Cursed how, exactly?" Angel asked.

"Once drawn, it can't be sheathed until it draws blood," Vivienne said. "Right?"

Yumi nodded, and Angel's eyes widened. "So that's what you meant, back on the rooftop."

Vivienne took a long pull of scotch. The buzz made all the feelings dull. "So," she said. "What do we know? What's the last thing you remember?"

Please don't say nuclear bomb. Please don't—

"We were at the table," Angel said. "Yumi, me, and—oh shit, where's *Claire*?"

"Focus," Vivienne said. "Tell me about Claire. Does she have powers?"

"Uh, I don't think so," Angel said. "She's just a high school girl."

You're both just high school girls. "What were you talking about?"

Angel shrugged. "I don't remember."

"Um," Yumi said. "I, uh, I was just talking about how hot you were."

"Yeah, I heard."

"You, uh, heard?" Yumi looked back toward the city, where they'd left the dragon, like maybe she could provoke it into squashing her.

"She got really weird about it," Angel said. "Like, I know she's Mormon, but—"

"Wait," Vivienne said. "She's *what?*"

"LDS," Yumi said. "It's a perfectly legitimate church."

"Not that," Vivienne said. "Is this girl, like, really sheltered?"

"I guess," Angel said. "I've never heard Claire swear. Or drink. Not even soda or coffee."

Yumi nodded. "Well, that's a Mormon thing, right?" she asked. "She always dresses super conservative. Like sweaters and stuff, even after Memorial Day."

"Uh huh," Vivienne said. "Did she seem ... surprised when you talked about me?"

"What do you mean?" Yumi asked.

"Maybe confused," Angel said. "Like, she thought Andre was the person Y was talking about."

Vivienne nodded. She narrowed her eyes, and the end of her mouth curled slightly.

"Oh damn, I know that look," Yumi said. "Whenever there's about to be a scene-break in the Supergroup comics, and Lady V ... you just figured something out, huh?"

Vivienne smirked.

~

Ashen wind swept across the rooftop of the burned skyscraper as the three of them landed—none too well, of course, but at least they didn't break anything this time.

It was dawn or so, but one would only know it by the blood-red sun barely peeking through the thick clouds of pollution over the mountains. Smoke rose in wafting clouds among the buildings, swirling around beams of darkness that descended from the sky to connect the beast to the dark heavens. Sure, that didn't look apocalyptic or anything.

"Team-up! Team-up!" The pink energy faded around them as the girl in black and pink shook out her arms and stretched—she wasn't used to carrying two people, and it showed. "Codenames?"

"I guess," said the girl in the black silks with the twin red capes. She grasped the handle of her katana, fairly leaking apprehension. Bloodmoon's old costume wasn't very warm, and she shivered slightly in the chill.

"Maybe you should add a coat," A-Girl said. "Ooh! Or an armored corset!"

"You mean make it *more* anime," Muramasa said.

"Obviously."

"Girls." Lady V adjusted her leather jacket over her own none-too-warm outfit. At least the safehouse had had one of her old armored costumes, and not the deep-V one. "Focus."

Obviously, the banter was to reassure each other, so she tried not to chide them too much. But there was an apocalyptic threat to deal with, and distraction was a recipe for disaster.

"So, the plan," A-Girl said. "Can we go over it one more time? Just to make sure."

Lady V noted her niece's fingers curling and uncurling against her tights, but she needn't have looked over. A-Girl was just as anxious as Muramasa. She had to remember these weren't experienced, veteran heroes. A-Girl mostly did photoshoots and music videos, and had fought maybe one or two low-level villains. Muramasa barely had a codename—she probably had never fought a real opponent. But both of them were here, and neither seemed about to flee. That was worth a lot.

"Team-up?" A-Girl asked.

"Definitely a team-up," Muramasa said.

"I'm not calling it that," Lady V said.

The dragon spread out below them, lounging in some kind of torpor, its many limbs spread around the city, claws jabbed into a number of buildings. It had chosen the magnificent glass library as its perch, and its massive bulk essentially crushed the building to twisted rubble and jagged, broken glass. The smoke that rose around the dragon came mostly from the contents of the library, which smoldered by proximity with its massive body. Several of its heads draped across nearby buildings, but the biggest one—the one with three horns—was tucked inside the building. As she had expected.

"Angel—" she started, then sighed. She rubbed her temples. "A-Girl, you fly around and cause as much havoc as possible to distract it. Meanwhile, ninja girl and I head down and cut the head off the dragon."

"Excuse me," A-Girl said. "It's *Muramasa*, not—"

"Are you sure?" Muramasa asked. "I can get in there, but you said your powers aren't working?"

Lady V bit her lip. It was true. Since that first moment with the dragon in the parking lot, she hadn't been able to absorb even a tiny shred of fear, much less shape anything with it. All she could do was read the emotions of the people around her, and so far, that was just two nervous high school girls. Neither of whom had the good sense to be afraid. Or maybe ...

There was deep, powerful emotion somewhere in this place, and she'd followed it to this spot. Darkness coiled around the crushed building below, and something hot and powerful beat within it, like a thudding heart. It might have been the dragon's heart, but Lady V didn't think so. It felt ... angry.

Out of the inner pocket of her jacket, Lady V pulled her silvery clawed gauntlet and slid it onto her left hand. Six-inch talons extended from her fingers, but that wasn't its greatest strength. She felt the claw's inherent power connect with her own, mostly quiescent magic, and tiny purple sigils appeared on its surface of its eldritch metal. She wasn't sure if that reassured her or not, but she would sure as shit pretend it did.

"I'm more than my powers," Lady V said. "A-Girl, go."

A-Girl nodded and took off in a burst of pink flames. She soared to the other side of the library, leaving a trail of pink energy that drifted down behind her. Two of the creature's nearest heads stirred, blood-shot eyes opening to look upon her.

Meanwhile, Muramasa had drawn out a folding bow, fired an arrow with a spiraling cord down toward the ruined library, and set the other end into the roof crenellation. She looked over at Lady V dubiously. "You can keep up?"

Lady V pulled out a clipping device with two handles. "No problem."

When Muramasa proceeded to dive off the rooftop, catch her scabbarded sword around the line, and zip down while holding the ends like a chin-up bar, Lady V started to see some problem. The girl flew down the line with such speed and balance, the capes looked like the wings of a bird fluttering around her.

"Just do it, Vengeance," she murmured, before Azazel would make a snarky comment. She tried not to think about what it meant for her mental health that she pre-emptively argued with the voice in her head before it even said anything.

She attached the clip to the cord and, before she could think better of it, kicked out over the empty air. And hell, was *that* a mistake.

She zipped along, raising her knees to reduce the pull on her arms, and could only watch as one of the dragon heads shifted out of the smoke under her and started to rise in her direction. The wan rays of sunlight caught on its crown, setting it to gleam hungrily, and one huge, red eye looked up at Lady V curiously. It was a disgusting thing, full of burst blood vessels and malignant rot, but its blade-shaped pupil narrowed even further and fixed upon her. The dragon's mouth started to open, flames and smoke leaking out ...

Which was when a semi-truck slammed into it from above, propelled by a pink streak of energy that zipped past the colliding, shattering impact.

The dragon gave a cry that was half-hiss, half-moan, and turned its attention on A-Girl, who soared up toward the broken heights of the skyscrapers around them. She smashed into a detached part of wall, sending it crumbling the rest of the way out over the street, and the dragon head smashed through the building lower, obliterating the top three floors in a burst of dust and debris. Overall, though, the many-headed beast didn't seem particularly bothered—the bulk of its body hardly shivered where it lay half-inside the collapsed building.

Lady V zipped the rest of the way down to the building, not too far behind Muramasa. The dexterous girl released with a flourish, turned a backflip in the air, and landed light on her feet, scabbarded sword held horizontal before her, ready to fight. Lady V, on the other hand, fared not so well: she let go of the zip line handles too soon, fell just long enough for her stomach to start climbing into her chest, then landed mostly on her feet, stumbled, and somehow managed to keep from faceplanting in a pile of burned books.

To her credit, Muramasa appeared not to notice. "What exactly are we looking for?" she asked.

Lady V pulled herself up, rubbing at her aching hip. Dropping twelve feet into a superhero pose was a young woman's game, especially one with the elastic joints of someone less retired. *Mostly* retired.

Her heart thudded between her ears, but not just because of the exertion. No, this place was indeed the source of all that emotion, and it set her off her ease.

"Just a second—" Lady V raised the gauntlet and drew a sigil of burning purple energy in the air. Her mind was already a mess of chaotic emotions, but the focusing spell let her narrow her senses. Her headache had grown worse, but she tried to push it aside.

The dragon's neck snaked around the interior of the hollowed-out building, the scales along its length scintillating with an eerie, unholy red light. It cast weird shadows across the burned walls and the ashen hulks of long-dead bookshelves.

The dragon was not the *source* of the light, however. That fell to the young woman in the center of the room: a red-haired girl of no more than fifteen, who knelt, hands clasped in fervent prayer. Which was appropriate, since she was wearing a nun's habit. Light shone from her as though from some sort of beacon, crimson as blood and dim. The light guttered even as they watched.

The biggest of the dragon's seven heads—the one with three horns and three corresponding crowns—hovered right in front of her, like a lurking cobra staring down a snake charmer in a magic act.

"Is that her?" Lady V started, even as Muramasa surged forward with a cry of "Claire!"

The dragon reacted instantly. While the prayers had seemed to captivate it, the presence of interlopers drew its attention away from Claire's efforts. The dragon roared, its jaws opening no less than three ways as though three mouths were super-imposed over each other, and it shot toward Muramasa before Lady V could even draw in breath to shout a warning.

But Muramasa reacted much faster than a semi-retired, hung-over ex-supervillain, and she sprang away even as the triple jaws snapped shut where she'd been half a second ago. The girl basically flew back, sword singing free of its lacquer scabbard, and waved away the gout of flame that erupted from the beast's mouth. It was damn impressive, sure, but Lady V knew Muramasa couldn't hope to outlast the dragon, magic ancestral sword or no.

Importantly, though, Lady V took one look at Claire Anderson praying desperately in the face of the beast and understood the whole thing. In retrospect, perhaps it should have been obvious—the jewels alone should have been a giveaway—but she'd blamed her diminished powers on a night of drinking, and the headache on the consequential hangover. And she was wrong.

Probably.

She hoped.

Shit.

"All right, that's enough, young lady." Lady V stepped out, arms crossed, talons tapping her leather jacket. "You've made your point."

The cowl or bonnet or whatever of the nun's habit rose, and Claire stared out with blood-shot pink eyes that were wide and innocent. "Point? What are you talking about?"

At that moment, the earth trembled underfoot, sending Lady V staggering. She managed to twist and land not flat on her face, but on her side, taking the impact on her hip. Which doubled the ache.

The chorus of booming trumpets that had shaken the ground sounded once more, and then as many voices joined in unison. "Fallen, fallen is Babylon the Great, Queen Harlot of Monsters—"

"Yeah, yeah," Lady V said. "It's not supposed to be taken *literally.*"

She was exhausted, and the heat and darkness in here drained her. It was like wandering in a fog, and it sucked all the moisture out of her skin.

As she climbed to her feet, Lady V saw Claire had gone back to her prayers, with even more urgency, and the light had dimmed to its lowest yet. There was a book in her hands: a thick tome with hundreds of pages of faded, yellow paper, marked with a golden ribbon. She was practically screaming her prayers now, all in something like Latin or something else Lady V didn't recognize.

"Load of good that'll do," she said under her breath. That was, after all, the problem.

The dragon's primary head had gone off in pursuit of Muramasa—Lady V could hear the whistle and cut of Muramasa's sword, the roar of flames and the harsh breath of an athlete reaching her limit—but other heads of the beast were snaking back into the building, descending toward her. She hoped A-Girl was all right, but either way, she hadn't succeeded in distracting them all. The multi-headed beast filled her with fear, and that confirmed her suspicions. If she could conquer it long enough to act on them.

Magic pulsed in her gauntlet, narrowly allowing her to climb back to her feet. Lady V gritted her teeth and faced the three dragon heads, which opened their multi-faceted mouths to slaver and hiss, producing sounds that sounded unsettlingly like her own name—the voice that of a demon lord she knew all too well.

"Vengeance," they said. *"Queen of Darkness. Empress of Monsters. Mother of Who—"*

"Yeah, we get it." Against every instinct inside her, Lady V turned away from the dragon to address Claire. "You think this is the first time someone has called me the Whore of Babylon? This isn't even the fifth, and those weren't all my sister." She held up the claw, relying on the protective barrier of purple energy it wove to hold the dragon at bay. It wasn't the threat—she hoped. "You can stop."

"I can't!" Tears streamed down Claire's cheeks. "I'm keeping us safe, don't you see? The beast won't attack. God's power—"

"This has nothing to do with any god," Lady V said, putting her hands wide to indicate the ruined world around them. "This biblical fan fiction is all you, kid. You, some bad literary scholarship, and your stunning imagination."

"What—?"

The girl wasn't getting it, and Lady V didn't have the time or wherewithal to explain it. She was about to collapse, and the world would crumble along with her. She had only the one chance.

"This is your destiny," Azazel said in her mind.

Fuck destiny.

Lady V stepped forward, the light warm on her skin, and brought her claws slashing down at the book. Claire's eyes widened, and she tried to snatch it back, but Lady V caught her by surprise. The gauntlet cleaved through the book with little resistance, and the thing broke apart into a cascade of leather and paper scraps, some of which crisped to ash and dissolved as they wafted to the floor.

A spark of hope rose in Lady V, and it let her shrug off her fear. And once she did that, as though a dam had broken inside her, Claire's fear flooded in—fear, anger, and *power.* Purple lightning danced around the gauntlet, then spread up her arm and around her torso. In its wake, the power sculpted plates of amethyst energy, armoring her arm and shoulder. It washed away the exhaustion and gave her back her strength. That, and that white hot bead of pure rage at the heart of Claire's emotional morass—it made her drunk with power.

Power that she could not *wait* to use.

The already fragmented ceiling of the former library smashed inward with a fall of rubble and A-Girl, flailing with pink energy, streaked downward and impacted with a small explosion that left a crater at least five feet deep. The girl lay panting, her costume scuffed and torn in places—she'd lost her helmet, too, and her golden hair tangled all around her pink-burning body.

And behind her came the last two of the seven dragon heads, fire dripping from their mouths.

"I've got it," A-Girl said as Lady V slid down into the crater. "Aunt V—"

"It's all right." Lady V laid a comforting hand on her shoulder. "I've got this."

When she looked up, her eyes brimmed with purple energy wrought of fear. All the fear of a dying world.

The great beast never had a chance.

One of the dragon heads came for her, jaws wide, and she smashed her fist up into its jaw with enough force to tear scales and shatter bone. The head spiraled away, flopping limply at the end of its long neck, and two more came for her, inhaling to breathe flame upon her from both directions. She shaped the power into a body shield around her gauntleted hand, and the fire parted around her, cracking the stone below her feet. She could feel the heat radiating through her shield, and see wisps of smoke rising from her coat. This was going to hurt.

A-Girl looked over at her, and Lady V got a little shot of fear from her niece for the first time. The spell wasn't just broken on her, but on the girls as well.

"Thanks, Angel." Lady V shaped the borrowed fear into a curved sword she grasped in her bare hand.

She said nothing else—had nothing to say. Instead, she acted.

Legs bent, Lady V shoved back the current of flame and leaped at one of the dragon heads. The creature reared back, but too slow: Lady V brought the sword stabbing upward, pinning two of its jaws shut, and the fire gushed all around them. She sensed the other head coming for her from behind, but the sword was still stuck in the dragon's head. She raised the shield ...

Abruptly, something dark moved in the firelight, leaping atop the dragon's neck, and then a circle of blood burst in the air. As she watched, the dragon's head revolved to one side, then slipped and fell to the floor, leaving only a bloody stump. The head turned black, shot through with purple veins like cracks, and started to dissolve—it was gone before it hit the floor, and the crown clanged off the paving stones. There was a symbol on that crown, Lady V noted: something like a question mark with tendrils extending from the base.

Muramasa, her costume mostly blackened, one of her two red capes burned away, leaped from the thrashing neck, turned a somersault in the air, and landed atop another of the creature's necks as the head came in to join the fray. The dragon roared, but a pink streak slammed into its chin from below, and A-Girl burst up and through it like a bullet fired straight at the sky.

Lady V smiled. The girls were up and fighting. The team-up was back on.

Not that she'd ever say that aloud.

The dragon was bleeding all over, great gouts of golden-yellow blood, such that gore and smoke rained from the sky, along with shards of glass and rubble. Its body had grown shadowed and black, shot through with yellow glowing cracks. The six lesser heads were either dead or occupied with A-Girl and Muramasa, leaving the three-jawed, three-horned, three-crowned head to salivate over Lady V and Claire. Oblivious to the threat, the girl cowered on the floor, picking vainly at the pieces of the discarded book that were disappearing. The creature turned on Claire, but Lady V raised her claw, burning with magic, to draw its attention. The purple flame reflected in the glassy black of its eyes.

"Bow before your Mother," she said, her words echoing around the shell of the building.

And the dragon did.

And even as it submitted, the dragon began to flake apart and dissolve into so much purple-black mist.

Like any other creation of her empathic projection.

Muramasa abruptly started to fall as the dragon neck she was standing on and hacking at with her Muramasa sword, but A-Girl shot at her and caught her in a flying tackle. They both tumbled to the floor in one of A-Girl's trademark clumsy landings, but they both seemed to be okay.

Lady V breathed a sigh of relief and looked to Claire. The girl still wore the nun habit, but it was starting to dissolve into her schoolgirl uniform. Her red hair had come undone, and it hung in a stringy mess around her tear-streaked face.

"It's ... it's all a lie. It's all fake." She looked to Lady V, eyes wide. "I always believed, but—"

The emotion coming off her wasn't what Lady V expected. It wasn't fear or confusion or anything like that. Instead ... Claire Anderson was *angry*. All the rage she had felt all this time, that was entirely hers. Buried deep and almost boiling up to the surface.

What if that anger could be unleashed?

Lady V almost reached out to hug the shivering girl, but she realized that might be a bit much. And might make everything a *lot* worse. Instead, she shrugged.

"I don't know if your god is real—or your devil or heaven or silver plates or whatever." She sighed. "But your faith is real, and that's gotta be enough."

Claire blinked. She clearly hadn't been expecting that. "What ... does that mean?"

"Fuck if I know." Lady V threw up her hands in exasperation. "Be a good person. Be kind to people. Embrace your queer sisters—don't freak out and end the world because your friend is—"

"Pan," A-Girl filled in.

"That one," Lady V confirmed. "Regardless, don't make any signs. Don't be a bitch. Maybe kiss a girl sometime. You might like it."

Claire blushed to the roots of her hair, face even redder than her mane.

Called it, Lady V thought, but said nothing. "Now look, can we get out of here? I need a drink—"

It hit her then. Simultaneously, she felt Claire suddenly let go, and a sucking emptiness opened in her stomach, like a black hole. Of a sudden, Lady V was hurtling back through the air and the world shrank and stretched around her and ...

~

68

They were back in Cain's Dive. The sun was setting out in the humid night, and the lights of passing traffic illumined the fogged windows. The three girls sat around the table at the front of the pub, blinking rapidly at each other. Vivienne stood at the end of the table, holding three menus, which she had clearly just collected. Somewhere in the back, the sounds of sizzling oil announced Andre firing up the deep fryer for Angel's tots.

Of all of them, Claire broke the silence first. "The Mediterranean plate, right, Yumi?"

"Uh." Yumi looked terrified. "Right. Yeah."

Angel said nothing. Her eyes flicked back and forth between her friends, and she was trembling.

"Sure—" Vivienne narrowed her eyes at Claire, but the redhead seemed oblivious. "Anything to drink?"

"Free refills on lemonade, right?" Claire asked.

"Right."

"Okay." Claire abruptly pushed away from the table, so suddenly Angel and Yumi both jumped—Angel actually put her hand through the upholstered surface of the booth. Claire grinned and rolled her eyes. "Don't freak out, I'm just going to powder my nose." She looked at Vivienne, her expression bored. "You have a bathroom, right?"

Vivienne pointed. "In the back. On your right."

The three of them watched her go, wave to Andre for confirmation, then disappear down the hall.

"Okay," Angel said. "What the hell was that?"

"A fearworld," Yumi said. "That's what it was, right? Like in the comics?" She shuddered. "I didn't realize it would feel so ... so *real*. Like a nightmare, except—"

Vivienne nodded. "I guess."

"You *guess*?" Yumi asked.

"Why would you put us in a fearworld?" Angel asked, her expression becoming annoyed. "If you wanted me to go away, you could have just said—"

"No," Vivienne said. "No, I—" She shook her head. "It wasn't me." She nodded toward the hall. "It was her."

"Claire?" Yumi and Angel asked in unison, then looked at each other.

"But ... she's just a girl," Angel said. "She doesn't have powers. At least—"

"And why doesn't she remember anything?" Yumi asked.

"Never underestimate the power of a repressed teenage girl." Vivienne checked her clothes, which had thankfully gone back to normal. She wasn't sure why, but that made her feel the most relieved. "Anything else?"

Angel took a long look at Yumi, who was looking away, and nodded with the sort of understanding only a clique of teen girls could manage. "I'll go check on Claire. Be right back."

Vivienne stood next to the table while Yumi sat there, entirely avoiding her gaze. She might be entirely acculturated American, but when she was embarrassed, she did the reserved Japanese woman extremely well. There was no fooling Vivienne's empathic senses, though.

So like her mother. Vivienne had to smile.

"You did good today, kid." Vivienne smiled. "Go to college, try the capes game, have some age-appropriate romances. You'll fuck them up, obviously—you're too much like me—but you'll have a hell of a time. Build a life for yourself. And—"

Abruptly, Yumi turned to Vivienne, mouth opening, inevitably about to say something she would regret, and Vivienne bopped her lightly on the head with the menus, startling her to silence.

Yumi blinked up at her.

Vivienne winked. "Maybe in ten years."

~

After the girls left, Vivienne headed out back to empty the trash, and that was when she saw it: the sign she'd seen in the Book of Revelation nightmare world, on the dragon's crown. It was chalked on the back wall of the Dive.

"Hnn," she said, and wiped it off with some soiled napkins.

A bag of trash thumped down next to her, and she almost jumped out of her skin. Andre grinned. "Hey. Something wrong?"

Vivienne shook her head. "I think ... I think something tried to push its way through here, but it got tangled."

"Tangled?" Andre asked.

"In that girl." She nodded. "Somehow, she stopped it coming in, and held it back. Shaped it."

"Like you do with fear?" Andre asked.

Vivienne shivered. "Yeah. Except with anger."

70

"Sweet Mormon Jesus," Andre said. "You realize how bad that could be?"

"Yeah." Vivienne bit her lip. "Figuring out what that was all about will have to wait. We've got more important things to worry about."

"When don't we?"

Vivienne nodded. She needed a goddamn drink.

Erik Scott de Bie is a sci-fi/fantasy author best known for his work in the Forgotten Realms, his Justice-Vengeance universe (which is at least partly contiguous with the Cobalt City universe), and his World of Ruin series. A veteran gamer, he has run thousands of hours of RPGs and has inevitably created his own game system for any property he loves. He also hosts the Westgate Irregulars twitch campaign as part of the Dungeon Scrawlers, a collective of geeky writers playing RPGs. He lives in Seattle with his wife and their entirely too adorable pets. Find him online at erikscottdebie.com.

Dead Souls

by Dawn Vogel

The burly bald guy manning the door at Club Sphinx took one look at the two masked women and gave them a faint nod. "Working?"

"Always," Terra said, smirking beneath her domino mask.

"We had a message from someone here about a potential problem?" Dulcamara asked, her face unreadable under the cover of her uncle's old luchador mask she wore as her costume.

Dulcamara and Terra Firma were two of Cobalt City's many superheroes. As students at Cobalt City University, they'd banded together with the other student heroes to establish their own form of campus and near campus security. The third member of their current team, Exspiravit, had created and managed an app for people to submit tips to the campus superheroes, and she'd sent them to Club Sphinx, just off campus, to assist.

"Ah, yeah," the bouncer said. "We've had a guy in pretty much every night, always leaves with a different person. Wouldn't have thought anything of it, but we haven't seen any of the people he's left with since then, and a couple of them are regulars."

Over the group's communications channel, Exspiravit said, "Ask about access to the external cameras, if they have them."

"Who would we need to talk to about getting access to your external building cameras?" Dulcamara asked.

The bouncer chuckled. "We've got about a week's worth of footage, if you want to sit in a tiny, cramped room and scan that for hours."

"Is it digital?" Exspiravit asked.

Dulcamara relayed the question, and the bouncer nodded. "Yeah, you need the IP or something?"

"Nah, we've got someone offsite to handle it. She prefers we ask before she hacks into your feed," Terra said.

The bouncer's eyebrows rose. "Oh. Ethical hacker. Yeah, permission granted."

"Thanks. So, is this guy here tonight?" Terra scanned the bar's dim interior, looking for anyone suspicious. Club Sphinx was a goth club, so there were plenty of people clad in all black, but that wasn't suspicious in and of itself.

The bouncer looked around as well, then nodded toward the back corner of the club. A waitress moved away from a corner booth, revealing a gaunt young man with jet-black hair falling in a shaggy mass around his head. Though he was seated, the visible parts of his body suggested he was tall, dressed in black with a silvery gray tie that gleamed in the low lighting.

"There we go," Terra said. "I'll signal if I need you."

Without waiting for Dulcamara's response, knowing the team leader would let her know if there was a problem, Terra approached the waitress, who was dressed in a black rockabilly-style dress. "I need to talk to your customer back there. Mind letting me take him his drink?"

"Suit yourself," the waitress said. "He ain't much of a conversationalist." She stepped behind the bar, grabbed a bottle of cheap domestic beer, and popped the top. "All yours."

"Thanks," Terra said. As she turned away from the bar, already her appearance was shifting to match the waitress's, down to her Bettie Page bangs and rhinestone Monroe piercing.

Dulcamara took in Terra's altered appearance and grabbed a stool at the bar. "Yell if you need me."

"Don't get too drunk," Terra teased her. Both of the heroes were just shy of their twenty-first birthdays, but as home to a large number of superheroes, Cobalt City had laws in place that allowed underage heroes in the pursuit of criminals to enter bars.

When she reached the booth, she slid the beer across the tabletop.

"Thanks," the guy replied, his attention gliding away from her.

Terra shot a glance at the sparsely occupied dance floor. "Looking for something in particular?" she asked.

The guy's brow furrowed. "Yes. But it doesn't concern you. I'll let you know when I want another beer."

Terra leaned on the table. "Aw, but I want to talk to you now."

"You're not what I'm looking for."

"No?" Terra shook her head until her hair came out red and choppy. "Better?"

The guy scoffed. "You always go around flaunting your powers like that? Like I told you. Not interested."

"But I'm interested in finding out what you're looking for." She crossed her arms over her chest and gave him a stern look. "If you don't feel like talking to me now, I think you'll open up if I press you enough."

The guy's gaze darted around to other parts of the bar, then locked on someone over her left shoulder. Terra turned to follow it.

Dulcamara was chatting with the waitress whose appearance Terra had borrowed. She was oblivious to this creeper's stare.

"You don't want a piece of that," Terra said. "She'll kick your ass six ways to Sunday."

"Who says that's not what I'm looking for?" he asked, arching an eyebrow at Terra for an instant before turning his stare back in Dulcamara's direction.

"Ew. Look, Stranger Danger. You're not her type."

"You a friend of hers?" He looked at Terra and her domino mask, now visible as she allowed her normal appearance to re-emerge. "Oh, of course. Superhero team-up, right?"

"Yep."

"Well, she's exactly what I'm looking for." The guy licked his lips. "What would it take to get you to introduce her to me?"

"Ugh, no."

"How about I spare you, then? You let me walk out of here with her, and you keep your soul."

"My soul?" Terra scoffed. "Bold of you to assume I have one."

He stared straight into her eyes. "You do. It's stunted, but you do."

A wave of revulsion slid over Terra. The guy wasn't looking away. She didn't think he was using a power on her, but she felt like she couldn't move.

A moment later, Dulcamara's vibrant and reassuring presence stood beside her. "What's up?" Dulcamara asked silently, using her subvocal communicator over the team channel.

The guy's gaze slid off Terra and onto Dulcamara. "You're exactly what I'm here for. Tasty."

"Tasty?" Dulcamara spat back. "Gross. I'm not food."

"Not for me—" He squinted at her. "—Handmaiden."

Beside Terra, Dulcamara tensed. Dulcamara's patron, Freya, occasionally took control of the hero's body without much warning, especially in situations of high danger. Terra gripped Dulcamara's hand, hoping her touch might keep Dulcamara present, preventing the goddess from making a wreckage of Club Sphinx.

It seemed to do the trick, or at least pulled some of the tension out of Dulcamara's body. "Get out," she said flatly. "Settle up your tab, tip your waitress heavily, and get out. Or you're going to have words with a goddess."

The guy's gaze slid between the two heroes in front of him, as though he was gauging his odds, but he finally nodded.

He slid to the side of the booth nearest Terra, and she stepped back, putting herself between him and Dulcamara, instinctively toughening her body in case he was using this as a ploy to attack them. But he continued out of the booth and toward the bar.

Terra and Dulcamara watched as he followed Dulcamara's instructions to the letter, even flashing the twenty-dollar-bill he left on the bar toward the two of them.

As he moved toward the door, Dulcamara subvocced, "Exie, our target's going out the front. Can you tag him?"

"No, but Jeeves can," Exspiravit replied. Jeeves was one of the drones she used to patrol the city and collect audio and visual data for the team. Barely bigger than a sparrow, Jeeves could also drop tracking chips with sculpted shells that worked like burrs, latching on to a person's clothing.

"Do it. We'll meet you at the lair," Dulcamara said.

~

Exspiravit's initial report hadn't been good. "I pulled the footage and found all the people who have left with this guy. So far, it's four for four on missing persons reports, filed after the point when he left with them."

"We let a serial abductor walk away," Dulcamara said, pounding a fist into her open hand. "And the bouncer even said he hadn't seen anyone that guy had left with. Ugh, we should have pummeled him there."

Now Dulcamara paced Exspiravit's lab, part of their "lair" that was more accurately a repurposed warehouse, gifted to them by a former resident of Cobalt City. Dulcamara's hands were balled into fists, as she waited for news of where the guy had gone.

Terra watched from her perch on one of Exspiravit's work benches, finally daring to break the tense silence. "Any guess on what that guy's deal was, aside from serial abductor?"

"You said he brought up souls," Dulcamara said, continuing to pace. "So probably a demon. Freya thinks frost giant, but to be honest, that's sort of her default assumption for anything that's not entirely human."

"His vitals read human," Exspiravit said, "not that I'm ruling out possession." She glanced away from her bank of monitors. "Can Freya do an exorcism?"

Dulcamara flicked her gaze toward the ceiling, then back. "Not in the strictest definition of such. But she says if he's possessed, she can deal with him."

Terra glanced at one of Exspiravit's monitors, which now had a pulsing red bullseye on it. "I think your tracker found something."

Exspiravit turned back to the screen. "Oh, that means he's exited his vehicle. North of North Morriston?"

Dulcamara frowned at the screen. "That's the bombed-out part of Old Innsmouth."

"Bombed out?" Terra and Exspiravit asked in unison.

"It happened during one of the World Wars, or in between, or something like that," Dulcamara said. "There was some sort of parasitic infestation in the reef, but the bombs weren't targeted accurately. I don't know the whole story, I just know my family lived out there back then, when they worked on the farms north of Cobalt City. Thankfully, they left before the bombing, or else I might not be here."

Exspiravit's fingers flew across the keyboard and a satellite overlay appeared beneath the bullseye, showing a pile of rubble sufficient to have been a larger building if it were intact. "I can cross-reference this with some older street maps—"

"No need," Terra said, pointing to an area to the left of the rubble. "Those look like tombstones to me. Where there's a cemetery, there's usually a church."

"And a church means there might still be a basement or an old crypt underneath," Dulcamara groaned. "And it would have been deconsecrated after the bombing. Perfect for demons."

Exspiravit flipped through a few staticky images on another of her screens, courtesy of the tracker Jeeves had dropped on the guy. The tracker's camera wasn't top of the line, but it worked well enough to let the heroes know what they might be getting themselves into. "Hang on, I might be able to ... uh, guys? Check this out?"

Dulcamara and Terra moved to flank Exspiravit's seat, squinting at the monitor. The image was grainy, with occasional bursts of a gray, pixelated mess. But the guy from the bar's voice was clear. "Mistress, I return empty-handed. My soul is yours for the sake of your sustenance."

The grainy background shifted, and Terra had an inkling of what they were looking at. It wasn't that the image was unclear. It was that something massive with pebbly and flaky gray skin took up the tracker's entire field of vision. When a sinuous neck brought a frilled serpentine head with gleaming golden eyes into view, Terra was the only one who found her voice.

"Dragon."

"Oh my god, a dragon?" Exspiravit squealed. "That's awesome!" Though she was a dozen years older than Dulcamara and Terra, she'd joined the superhero world later in life, when she realized her hacking and tech skills made her a valuable assistant to heroes. She got giddy over the strangest things.

The feed flickered to pixels one last time, then showed a toothy maw much larger than the guy from the bar's head. Then it went black.

At that, Exspiravit shoved back from her workstation, her rolling chair nearly clipping Terra's toes. "That dragon ate a guy."

"Yeah," Dulcamara said softly. "That thing's ... massive. They're not usually in our ... realm, I guess is the closest word, but—" She trailed off, shaking her head. "Sorry, Freya's screaming at me in Old Norse. Malice striker? Devourer. Nithhoeggr."

"That one I know," Terra said. "Dragon at the base of Ygdrassil, right?"

Dulcamara nodded. "Freya's going to check and see if it's missing."

"What are we supposed to do against a dragon who eats people?" Exspiravit asked, her eyes wide.

"Punch it, I guess," Terra said. "I mean, I assume they're punchable."

"Sure," Dulcamara said, "but if it's Nithhoeggr, we're going to need a lot more firepower. We're talking about a god-like creature."

"We're talking about a dragon," Terra replied. "I sort of expect they're all god-like to mere humans. Okay, we know it's big, but can we get more specific than really big?"

"Umm, I can run some diagnostics," Exspiravit said, rolling her chair back to the workstation. She focused on the keyboard, muttering something unintelligible under her breath, but she seemed to relax as she began working with the data.

"What are you thinking for firepower?" Terra asked Dulcamara quietly.

"Stardust? Velvet?" Dulcamara named off a couple of Cobalt City's strongest heroes.

"Okay, but I don't think we're on 'call up Stardust or Velvet and get them to help us' terms, right?"

"Probably not. I could round up a few people from school, like Mark or Janella, maybe, but not the big guns. Not unless we're staring down a threat to the city proper."

"If this dragon has agents fishing for souls in Cobalt City, that's a threat to the city, right?"

Dulcamara shook her head. "Not the same level. We can deal with agents of a dragon. Going back to the source seems suicidal. Unless we've got some sort of edge I'm not thinking of."

Terra paused, glancing back at Exspiravit's monitor. "Hang on, can you zoom at all?"

"Yeah, but it's not going to improve the image quality," Exspiravit said, enlarging a bit of the screen that went from showing a lumpy gray mass to a blurrier lumpy gray mass.

Terra pointed at the screen. "But there's something shiny there, in the midst of all the gray. Maybe blood, or some other sort of bodily fluid?"

Dulcamara peered at the screen. "Maybe, yeah. It looks wet."

"What if it's already weakened, somehow? Do you think we could take it then?" Terra asked.

"You seriously want to fight this thing? Just the two of you?" Exspiravit asked. "Did you miss the part where that dragon *ate* a guy? In one bite?"

"Maybe we can talk to the dragon first," Terra suggested. "Because how cool would it be if we could talk to a dragon? Maybe it ate that guy from the bar because he was a jerk."

Dulcamara shrugged. "Sure, that's a good start. Guess we're going to go talk to a ... well, Freya says it's not Nithhoeggr. Probably."

"See?" Terra said, grinning. "Piece of cake."

~

By the time Terra and Dulcamara reached the collapsed church in Old Innsmouth on Terra's motorcycle, Exspiravit's drones were already there.

"I can't get a good sensor read because of the rubble, but I sent Jeeves in, and there are about two dozen people in addition to the dragon. Most of them seem to be attending it. It's injured, but I don't know enough about dragon physiology to say how injured." Exspiravit paused. "Also, I thought dragons should be a lot prettier than this one is."

"What, like with big eyelashes and fancy makeup?" Terra asked.

"No, just not so grimy looking. I don't think this dragon's ever had a bath."

Dulcamara sighed. "Okay, I'll focus on suppression and restraint for any over-enthusiastic dragon worshipers or whatever they are. Exie can monitor the situation, and Terra can do the talking."

"Roger," Exspiravit said. "Do we need a team-up name for this operation?"

Terra groaned. "I already know you're going to suggest Triple Threat."

"Duh," Exspiravit replied.

"Fine, whatever you say, Exie," Dulcamara said, shaking her head subtly at Terra. The group had been through this discussion or argument several times before, and Dulcamara didn't think it was worth fighting over a temporary team name. Even if the two heroes on the ground were working with Exspiravit more and more frequently.

The two young women made their way into the ruined church and down the first set of stairs they found. The lower level had no ceiling covering much of it, but the moonlight didn't quite penetrate to this level, making it dim and treacherous to navigate.

"There's a small group of heat signatures to the left," Exspiravit announced over the comms.

"Okay, then that's me," Dulcamara replied. "Hold for a minute and I'll rejoin you." She slipped off in the direction Exspiravit had indicated, cautiously picking her way across the brick-strewn floor.

Almost as soon as she disappeared from Terra's view, the sounds of shifting bricks and stone came from where Dulcamara had gone. That was followed by something that sounded like a heavy rope being whipped around, and a moment later, Dulcamara reemerged from the archway she'd entered. "Four down," she reported over the comms channel. "Definitely a cult of some sort, though I can't tell if they've been magically coerced or if they're doing this for fun."

"There are more, but they're not clustered, as best as I can tell," Exspiravit replied. "But without input from the bug Jeeves dropped, I can't tell for sure what's below you. Jeeves didn't go very far down. I didn't want him to become dragon food."

Dulcamara peered into the dim surroundings. "I don't see any way to get down, yet."

Terra shifted her eyes through several spectrums of light until she spotted a wide hole gaping in the middle of the floor. "Ooh, I found one way."

"What's up?" Dulcamara asked.

"There's a hole over there," Terra said, pointing.

A drone whirred overhead, flying toward the hole Terra was watching, and a moment later, Exspiravit said, "The dragon is straight down from there."

Dulcamara grinned. "So let's drop in." She gestured at some of the roots nearby, and they braided themselves together with some new growth that her plant manipulation powers seemed to have inspired. The bits of roots and vines coiled into a rope, solidly anchored to one of the still-standing pillars on this level. "Terra, care for a ride?"

Terra shapeshifted to about half her size and leapt onto Dulcamara's back, holding on like a child getting a piggyback ride. Dulcamara grabbed the vine rope and leapt toward the hole.

The two heroes landed in a cloud of brick and stone dust, Terra tucking into a roll as she dislodged herself from Dulcamara's back, but the dragon's golden eyes fixed on them despite the haze.

"Who dares disturb my slumber?" the dragon bellowed.

"Dulcamara and Terra Firma," Terra replied. "And how would you like to be addressed?"

"'Mistress' seems to be the best your paltry language offers. Unless your feeble tongues can manage 'Vostra Maestà, Divora'."

Terra hesitated a moment, until Exspiravit said, "Italian. Your Majesty," over the comms.

"Why are you here, Your Majesty?" Terra asked.

"I have been called upon to render service to one who has me in his debt. I shall not speak his name."

"Is it He-Who-Shall-Not-Be-Named?" Exspiravit asked over the team's comms channel.

"Worse, probably," Dulcamara replied.

"And what would this patron have you do?" Terra asked Divora.

"Wait, strengthen myself, prepare for his call. Then, assist him in his invasion of this—" She trailed off. "—how does he call it, 'Iteration'?"

Terra turned toward Dulcamara, even though she didn't have to look at her to communicate. "Sound like anyone we know?"

"Dunno," Dulcamara said, punching her right fist into her left palm, "but I'm not a fan of invasions, especially by nameless patrons."

Terra took that as her signal to rush toward Divora, her hands forming into blades and her gaze fixed on one of the many glistening welts on the dragon's skin.

The ridge above one of the dragon's eyes raised, like she was arching an eyebrow. And then she transformed into a long, slender, eel-like creature that bolted away from the heroes and through a narrow crevice in the wall.

"On it!" Terra exclaimed aloud.

Dulcamara shouted over the comms, "Be careful! I'm going to deal with suppression of these ... dragon cultists. That's weird even for Cobalt City."

Terra scrambled through the crevice in Divora's wake, shifting into something long and slender as she went. On the other side, no floor rose up to meet her scrabbling feet, a dark void yawning beneath. She stretched what was left of her arms and transformed them into wings, becoming a winged snake-like creature, not too different from the form Divora had taken.

Divora had lengthened the distance between her smooth, sinuous eel form and Terra's clumsier version of the same.

Terra refined her form as she flew, getting closer and closer to a replica of Divora's form. The new form flew more smoothly, but it didn't grant her the necessary additional speed.

Improvising, she shifted muscle mass into her wings. When they flapped the next time, they produced a rush of wind and a burst of forward motion.

Divora shifted, and Terra spotted one of the dragon's golden eyes glaring in her direction. Then she shifted back to her gargantuan scaled form with mighty wings. "So, you wish to fight me?"

Terra tried to keep the exhaustion from her rapid-fire transformations from her voice. "No, but I can't let you get away."

Divora snorted. "Fool."

Terra watched the dragon's movements. It was subtle, but it seemed as though she'd reached some sort of outer wall of this massive underground chamber, perhaps solid enough that Divora couldn't escape in that direction. In addition, rivulets of fluid now mottled the dragon's scales, giving them a shine they'd previously lacked.

Was this shapeshifting as hard on Divora as it was on Terra?

That gave her an idea.

Terra flew toward Divora, taking a slight angle that gave Divora plenty of room to evade her, so long as the dragon flew back in the direction they'd come.

It was a cat and mouse maneuver, with Terra in the superior position, but Divora took the bait.

"Bringing her back your direction," Terra murmured over the comms.

"What? Why?" Dulcamara asked. "I've got my hands full!"

"Because I think she might be slowing down. And because if I transform too much more, I'm going to pass out."

"Go smaller, if you have to," Dulcamara suggested. "You said that's easier than going bigger."

"They both take it out of me, though," Terra said. "Do you think you can you handle a weakened dragon?"

"I can deal with these worshippers or I can deal with her," Dulcamara said. "Or I can let Freya out to handle everything. But you know what her methods look like."

"Yeah, we're going to need to get more information out of Divora," Terra said. "Okay, I'll see what I can do."

Now that Terra wasn't chasing her at full speed, Divora had turned to fly backward, all her attention on Terra. "You're planning something, aren't you, little one?"

"Probably," Terra said. "But so are you, and if you won't tell me your plan, why should I tell you mine?"

Divora snarled. "Or I could end this silly game and crush you and your friend like bugs."

Terra smirked. Taunting a dragon might prove to be the dumbest thing she'd done, but it was hard to resist. "Can you? Really?"

As she spoke, she shapeshifted, compacting her body smaller and smaller. At the size of a fat city pigeon, Terra knew she packed enough strength to break through plywood.

She suspected an injured, Coil-travelling dragon had some weak points. Especially if she dove through one of the wounded areas with fangs and claws added on to her little bullet-shaped bird form.

Terra hurtled through the air toward Divora.

The dragon looked confused by Terra's sudden change in tactics, leaving her wide open to Terra's improvised attack.

Terra tried to ignore the squelching feeling of flying through another body. For a brief second, she considered shifting back to her normal form to wreak more havoc on Divora from the inside, but she reconsidered as a wave of fatigue swept through her. It would suck to be stuck in human form inside of an angry, injured dragon.

She punched out the other side of Divora's body, shaking off some of the gore to maintain her flight trajectory. She was unable to make out much more than the fine point of light where the crevice led back to the room where she'd left Dulcamara. Terra flew toward the light, the dragon still hot on her metaphorical heels.

She plunged through the crevice and tumbled to the ground beside Dulcamara, her body reverting to its natural form, still stained with dragon's blood.

"Oh my gods," Dulcamara said aloud. "Terra, what happened?"

"Incoming," Terra croaked, pointing back toward the crevice, before she passed out.

~

Terra woke to someone half-chanting and half-shouting in a Nordic language, and she wondered if she'd fallen asleep studying while Dulcamara was listening to Norse metal.

Then she recalled the dragon, Divora, chasing her, realized her mask was still on, and started to sit up.

"Stay low," Exspiravit said across the comms channel. "Dulcamara's channeling Freya and they're trying to banish the dragon."

"So we're not going to talk to Divora?"

"No, we got enough information while she was swearing she'd sooner die than give up the King's secrets.

"Oh," Terra replied. "Which King?"

"The jaundiced one, I think," Exspiravit replied. "You're not supposed to say his name aloud, or he can see your thoughts or something gross like that."

"Great. How's the banishing going?"

"Almost done, I think. Then we need to ward something so the dragon won't come back."

"Cool, so magic stuff?"

"Yeah, magic stuff."

"Then I'm going to lay here on the cool, cool ground for a while." Terra closed her eyes for a moment, then they flew open again. "Wait, what happened with the dragon cultists?"

"Subdued, for the most part. Tied up with vines and stuff."

"Do they need checking on?"

"No." Exspiravit paused. "Wait. Maybe? There's some energy flowing off them toward Divora—"

Terra frowned, trying to figure out what an energy transfer to the dragon might mean. The guy in the bar had been talking about souls. She groaned. "Divora feeds on souls."

"In that case, yes. I think you should get them out of her, um, soul-siphoning reach?"

Terra forced herself into a sitting position and took stock of the situation.

Dulcamara, wreathed in golden armor and helm with a pair of transparent cats weaving between her legs, stood facing Divora, screaming the words Terra had woken up hearing. The dragon writhed with each word, though she didn't seem to be going anywhere, possibly because of the influx of power from her followers, who were tied up in a large group on the other side of the room.

"Okay, I'm going to get some of these cultists out of here."

"I figured out where the stairs are, but shouldn't you be careful with your shapeshifting?" Exspiravit asked. "You *just* passed out."

"I don't have to shapeshift to move people," Terra said, grinning. As she rose, she stumbled and shook her head. "Especially in my current state."

"I'm monitoring your vitals," Exspiravit said, "but so help me, if you do pass out, you're going to have to wait until Dulcamara and Freya are done."

Terra approached the group of cultists, bound hand and foot and clustered together. "If any of you plan to die for Her Majesty, you wanna save me the trouble and lay on your sides? Anyone who doesn't want to die, I'll give you a hand up, and then you keep going until you can't hear my friend's voice anymore."

Three of the cultists rolled to their sides, while the others struggled to get to their feet.

Terra shapeshifted her fingernails into talons—a small enough change that she didn't fear for her conscious state—and began cutting the vines that held the cultists feet together as she helped them off the ground.

By the time she reached the last three cultists, two of them were struggling to sit again.

"Changed my mind," one of them said, eying Terra's talons. "I'll go."

"Me too," the other said.

The third cultist remained on their side, glaring defiantly at Terra.

"I'm not going to let you die," she said, slinging an arm around the cultist's waist and tossing them over her shoulders in a fireman's carry and heading toward the stairs. "Letting her kill you would be idiotic on both our parts."

The cultist tried to struggle against Terra's grasp, but she diverted strength to her arms and shoulders, keeping the cultist restrained as they left the basement of the church.

Behind her, a shuddering sound followed by a squelching pop drew Terra's attention.

"Oh, are we done?" she asked over the comms.

"Yes, the dragon's been banished. Nothing but the warding to finish," Dulcamara replied. "Glad you're awake."

"What do we do with the cultists?"

"Stern warning about rethinking their life choices?" Dulcamara suggested. "We don't have any evidence of crimes. They might have abducted people like the creeper from the bar was trying to do, but unless any of them admit to anything of the sort, I guess they're free to go."

Terra nodded. "I think I can regale them with a few tales of why they shouldn't continue on this life of dragon worship, with a few 'your mother would be disappointed in you' stories for emphasis."

"Ooh, I've got some good examples of that too, if you want to put me on broadcast," Exspiravit said cheerfully.

"Excellent," Dulcamara said. "Then we'll see you upstairs in a bit. Good job, both of you."

Terra grinned. "Agreed. Good job—" She grimaced but continued. "Good job, Triple Threat."

———

Dawn Vogel writes a little bit of everything, but she has a special place in her heart for the heroes of the Cobalt City universe. By day, she edits reports for historians and archaeologists. In her alleged spare time, she runs a craft business, co-runs a small press, and tries to find time for writing. Her steampunk adventure series, *Brass and Glass*, is available from DefCon One Publishing. She is a member of Broad Universe, SFWA, and Codex Writers. She lives in Seattle with her husband, author Jeremy Zimmerman, and their herd of cats. Visit her at historythatneverwas.com.

Battlelines

by Nathan Crowder

My knees popped and there was a twinge in my back when I stood that reminded me that just three days previous, I had a building dropped on me. I told Elizabeth it was a small building, but getting hit with anything big enough to be considered "architecture" was sub-optimal. My shields absorbed the damage, but getting out from under a few tons of concrete and rebar was a hell of a lot easier when I wasn't forty-six.

I padded down the corridor to the armory, motion sensors triggering the lighting panels in the ceiling as I went. Dragons had been appearing around Cobalt City, causing a variety of problems recently. Thus far, I'd missed all the excitement. Newer, younger heroes and old Protectorate friends Wild Kat and Velvet alike had gone toe-to-toe with the dragons. And try as I might, the excitement had been long over before I could get there each and every time. It reminded me of when the Protectorate dealt with splinter realities a dozen plus years before. We'd gotten dropped into some medieval fantasy version of Cobalt City and a dragon showed up, only to get knocked unconscious by Velvet before I could get a Starbolt warmed up.

Far as I was concerned, I was due. And the huge, red, fire-breathing bad boy in the air now was mine. I called dibs. Thankfully, there weren't many flying heroes likely to beat me there. Maybe that Johnny Turbo character. Or that witch I'd tangled with in the rail yards a few months ago.

What was her name? Bog Witch? If she beat me to the punch, maybe it was time to hang up the Stardust armor.

"What's the current tracking?" I asked my computer as the armory door hissed open.

"Over the bay and circling back for another pass," the disembodied and lightly British voice said in my ear.

"Anyone else in the air?"

"Target is unengaged. However, Delta flight 1137 from D.C. is inbound, and target is adjusting to intercept. No other heroes spotted."

Crap. That was a new wrinkle. I opened the charging drawer and plunged my hands into the waiting gauntlets. The Stardust suit began swiftly unfolding from the gauntlets to cover my body. I snatched the helmet off its stand and slammed it down over my head. The systems display sprang to life across the gold-tinged visor. All systems were green. I stepped into the boots and they closed around my feet and ankles.

"Suit synched and online," the computer confirmed. "Stand clear for deployment portal."

The wall before me irised open, revealing an overcast sky and what used to be a great view of downtown until developers put in a sixty-story mixed use tower two blocks south of Starcom Plaza. They had a gym on the same level as my main terrace. I could watch people on the treadmills when sipping my morning coffee if I wanted to.

"Jaccob?" Elizabeth's voice sounded in my ear piece. "Why is the deployment portal open?"

"Dragon. Can't talk," I said, blasting out into the afternoon sky.

"Jaccob Stevens, you know the doctor said you needed to rest your back."

She didn't tell me to turn around. She didn't tell me to stop. Liz wasn't like that. She gave me the warnings. Told me the odds. Let me make the decisions myself. And yes, the doctor had told me to rest my back. If I hadn't been alternating ice and heat while downing Ibuprofen, I wouldn't have made it off the sofa. If it had been a bank robbery, or high-speed pursuit, or literally anything other than a dang dragon, I wouldn't have budged.

But a dragon was another matter. And with it about to pick a fight with a packed airplane, it was the right decision.

I caught a view of the scaly bastard cutting a furrow through the clouds. The HUD in my helmet tagged it, locking on target, giving me a readout in the bottom right of my visor. Tip to tail, this thing was over 250 feet long with a wingspan to match. If it decided to get in the weeds—and by weeds, I meant the towers of downtown Cobalt City—it was going to be carnage. It had already made a pass at the Pyewacket Building, melting the statue of Arnold Pyewacket on the roof, as well as setting the corporate penthouse on fire.

"Show trajectories for myself, dragon, and airplane. Plot contact countdown," I said, rewarded seconds later with a map overlay on my visor. I had time, provided I could get its attention. I goosed the boot jets up another notch, since speed was more important than maneuverability out in the wide open. As the gap closed, I fired off a few Starbolts, hitting the dragon once in the side and once on a wing.

Its massive head turned my direction just long enough to let out a gout of flame the length of a football field. My shields compensated for it. I felt the heat, and broke out in an immediate sweat, despite the coolant layer in the suit. But at least I wasn't cooked-in-can like tuna.

It also wasn't enough to get the dragon's full attention. The airplane was either big enough to present as a confusing threat or more substantial meal. I didn't know. Who knows why dragons do what they do?

I toggled on the loudspeaker and blasted out the only real warning I was going to attempt. "Turn around and return to where you came from and I won't have to hurt you!"

If it heard and understand me, it called my bluff and kept on toward the jet liner.

And it had been a bluff. Sort of. My two Starbolts hadn't even scratched it.

"Deploy probes," I said, followed by two hand-sized automated probes launching from a rack on my back. "Scan for weak spots, loose scales, anything," The pair of golden disks zipped ahead to do an extensive reading on the target from a safe orbit. While I waited for results, I pushed on, closing the distance and targeting the veiny wing membrane of the dragon's left wing.

The dragon roared in pain, and I was relieved by the size of the hole I'd punched in the wing. When it tottered in the air, I had an immediate panic that I'd screwed up. Blowing a giant lizard out of the sky and flattening a few blocks of North U would not be good for my press right now. Would anyone be surprised? Other than the people in the homes and businesses that got pancaked? Sadly, no. But I needed to avoid that. I was actually relieved when the dragon wheeled around to face me.

My shields took the brunt of that gout of flame as well, but internal temps were up fifteen degrees, and the suit coolants were protesting. I couldn't take this all day. The shields could keep the fire itself away for the most part, but the superheated air was still at risk of cooking me alive if this kept up.

I popped it in the face with two more Starbolts and angled back out toward the bay. It took the bait and raced after me. My pair of golden probes remained locked onto the dragon, spinning in a graceful orbit, scanning and interpreting every spare bit of data they could get and feeding them back to the display in my visor. The good news: I'd already proven the wings were vulnerable. But the good news pretty much ended there. The rest of the beast was covered in scales that either reflected or absorbed most of the force from the Starbolts.

Another gout of flame licked at my heels, shot up my body from behind. It felt like I'd stepped into an industrial oven. Or a black car left out in a Florida parking lot all day.

I sent another set of instructions to the probes. "Figure out how it's making fire." I prayed there was a scientific explanation. Science I could work with. If it was magic, it would just confirm that magic sucked and wanted me dead. "And give me a warning when it's about to try and cook me next time."

"Fire appears to be a chemical process generated in a bladder inside the creature's neck," a somewhat familiar male voice said in my helmet's ear piece.

"Who is this and how did you hack my suit?" I asked, fearing I already knew the answer.

"Wrecker of Engines, and I didn't hack your suit. I hacked your drones. I wouldn't disrespect you by hacking your suit unless I had to." Despite the intrusion, the Wrecker sounded polite. I'd known he was around the scene for a few years, but we'd never met in person. I strongly suspected he'd gotten access to several of Starcom's telecommunication satellites but could never prove it. Last I'd heard, he was holed up somewhere in Asia running tactical superhero strike teams.

"Why are you in my systems?"

"Not the point. Get ready to dodge hard left in 3, 2, 1," he said calmly.

I instinctively took a hard barrel roll to the left as a huge gout of dragon fire roasted the air where I'd been mere seconds before. "Thanks. Now answer the question."

"Would you believe if I said I just happened to be in the neighborhood?"

The Cannonade passed beneath me with open water ahead. Another thirty seconds, and I could drop this dragon somewhere safe and hope the fall and the waters of the bay would do the rest.

"I don't believe you. A little bird told me you're in, I'm going to say ... Hong Kong?"

"Heh. Hard right in 3, 2, 1."

I executed another hard barrel roll, narrowly avoiding getting cooked again. Somewhat more troubling, I felt it tweak the muscles in my back along the right side. The jolt of pain caused me to ease off the throttle for a second. According to my visor display, the dragon took the opportunity to pull a lot closer to me than I was happy with. If I took the time to look behind me, it might slow me enough to put me between the thing's teeth.

My back burned. I remembered when I'd bent over to put a plate in the dishwasher the previous day and my back locked up entirely for a few painful minutes. If that happened here, I'd be a spicy sky raisin for this giant lizard.

I fired blindly behind me a few times with my gauntlets, the Starbolts glancing harmlessly off the dragon's scales. Preparing for the end game, I started another blast charging in each gauntlet, pushing the capacity toward the redline.

"As for Hong Kong," the Wrecker of Engines continued, "I love the city, but it was starting to feel claustrophobic. And America's political situation, with President Prather trying to bring vigilantes in line, made Cobalt City a little problematic as well. No. I'm somewhere with room to operate, room to grow, room to see the big picture. And the big picture is that we have a dragon problem."

I checked my drop zone. Nothing below me but the cold waters of Cape Cod. It was now or never. "And here I thought you were watching what was going on here. I'm just about to solve our dragon problem."

I rolled to my back, looking behind me quickly to let out the two super-charged Starbolts right at the dragon's left wing, shredding it. My victory cry was cut short by the dragon's massive head snaking out and snapping closed around me.

First thing: the inside of the dragon's mouth smelled like sulfur and hot, wet garbage as the huge, black tongue mashed me around, trying to force me back into its gullet.

Second thing: I was damn glad the teeth missed me by three inches, because I wasn't sure my shields could have handled it. They could barely handle being tongued to death by this medieval menace.

Third thing, and perhaps most important: my entire back chose that exact moment to seize up on me. It was the very definition of bad timing.

At least my onboard altimeter showed that both the dragon and I were currently plummeting toward the water.

"Was that intentional?" Wrecker asked over the headset communicator.

"Not exactly," I grunted through clenched teeth. Was it me, or was it getting hot in here?

"The dragon is preparing another fire blast. Possibly to clear you out."

There was no barrel rolling out of this situation. It didn't leave me with a lot of options. "Maneuver seventeen," I said to my onboard computer. Automated contingencies clicked into operation. I cut loose with both gauntlets in the general direction of the chemical sack that produced the flame in the dragon's throat, hoping the inside was less armored than the outside. A fraction of a second after the Starbolts cleared the gauntlets, my armor and shields went full "Pillbug" mode, covering me in as much armor and shields as my suit could generate.

It was a purely defensive option, turning me into an armored capsule with chewy meat in the middle. I couldn't fly or shoot. But with my back muscles trying to relocate vertebrae and sever my spine, at least from the feel of it, it wasn't like I could do much anyway.

When the dragon's head exploded, I was shot out and across the waters of Cape Cod like a golden Tic Tac.

"Was *that* intentional?" Wrecker of Engines asked.

"It worked, didn't it?" I shot back.

"Yes. But will you be in any shape to help with the others?"

I wasn't sure I heard him right, as I was currently skipping across the water at high velocity like a flat thrown stone. But I was sure he said "others." In my protective little capsule, I checked the incident reports that my telecommunication satellites generated by scraping broadcasts, data streams, and phone calls for keywords.

If the calculations from aggregate reports were correct, eleven more dragons had appeared in the vicinity of Cobalt City since I'd started tangling with the red dragon.

"Where are they all coming from?"

"Short answer is other dimensions," Wrecker of Engines said, but his tone suggested even he wasn't happy with that answer. "Longer answer, the things are like snowflakes. No two are alike. And I don't think they're from the same place. The energy signatures when they appear are too varied. It's almost like someone posted our address on a dragon bulletin board and invited everyone to swarm."

I looked at the reports coming in across my feed. Swarms of small winged serpents tearing through Lafayette Park. Giant serpentine dragon surfacing in the Puckwudgie River beneath Harkness Street Bridge. Skeletal dragon clawing from the earth near abandoned Harrowhill Cemetery on the western border of the city. A giant black dragon spewing poison gas from the top of Mill Hill in south Karlsburg, while a trio of pink dragons were menacing Little Warsaw in north Karlsburg. More reports coming in every minute.

"It's an invasion," I said, remembering the huge interdimensional breach in Lafayette Park in the summer of 2004 that led to the creation of the Protectorate. It had been my big debut in Cobalt City. And now, fourteen years later, dealing with my own tired carcass was as big a challenge as pushing back the invaders had been then. I couldn't do it. I couldn't push back the deadly lizards myself, and the Protectorate had been a dead dream for over a decade now.

"Not an invasion," Wrecker said. "It's why I hijacked your satellite. I needed a good overhead view to coordinate and confirm. I wanted to make sure this wasn't like the psychic trans-dimensional infection that caused the Mother Goose Incident in 1934. But this isn't coordinated enough to fit any of those scenarios. In fact, every scenario I've been able to crunch and run through the algorithms has come up question mark except one."

"And that is?"

"Chaos. The only thing that makes sense is to create chaos."

My inertia had slowed enough that I risked turning off Pillbug mode. I dropped into the water for a few seconds before my jet boots kicked in and sent me flying back toward Cobalt City on the horizon. I could see a long, winged shape coiling sinuously through the sky above Clark Tower in the Cannonade. It was hard to tell from this distance, but I could swear it was feathered instead of scaled.

"Not chaos," I said, knowing the truth in my gut. "Madness."

"Madness?" Wrecker of Engines echoed. "You think the King in Yellow is behind this?"

"I think it bears tracking down Louis Malenfant and smacking some answers out of him."

In my head, I started plotting out something like a game plan. Blast through the feathered serpent and hope I could one-punch it. Move on to Little Warsaw and tangle with the trio there. Maybe I'd still be alive to take on the dracolich on Mill Hill.

"Malenfant vanished off the face of the earth three months ago," Wrecker of Engines said. "I've been looking for him, and he was last spotted heading down an alley and into a bar that doesn't exist anymore."

"Like, closed?"

"Like vanished. Some place called Dante's."

I knew the place. It was a hell bar, not entirely of this world. Interdimensional nuisance Darla Spider had used it as a hangout when she'd tried messing with me and my family back in the day. If Malenfant had entered Dante's, there was no telling where he was now, but it almost certainly wasn't this dimension anymore.

Added to that, more dragons kept appearing. By my count, there were twenty-three sightings in the greater Cobalt City area alone, along with a few others around the world.

The advantage of having gone Pillbug to be launched like a bullet from a gun was that my back seemed to be cooperating for now. I still favored one side, though, out of an abundance of caution, and had to keep course correcting to keep from drifting left. I drew a bead on the big feathered serpent and overcharged a pair of Starbolts. One coordinated blast, then try to punch through wherever I'd shot, and maybe that would be enough. Or maybe this was it. Only one way to find out. "At least I'll go down fighting."

"About that—" Wrecker of Engines said playfully.

Before I could fire off my Starbolts, a humanoid figure that my sensors said was around the same temperature as the surface of the sun punched through the dragon from head to tail at supersonic speeds, incinerating it in the air. As I watched, the brilliantly burning figure angled up and away over the city toward what I could only expect was another dragon.

"Who the hell is that?"

"Goes by Bluestar. He's new," Wrecker of Engines said. "I did say I hijacked your satellite to coordinate, didn't I? You're not alone here, Jaccob. The cavalry is here."

I pulled up to a stop, hovering over the Cannonade as ash from the feathered serpent rained down upon historic buildings. I looked at the dragon reports again.

Trust him or not, the kid hadn't been lying. All over the city, heroes had risen to the challenge in a coordinated effort to push the dragons back. I didn't even recognize everyone. For every familiar face like Wild Kat and Velvet, there were at least two heroes or, for all I knew, villains, that hadn't appeared on my radar yet.

"How is this possible?"

"While other heroes were going to ground because of Prather and his goons, I've been building something."

"Your surgical strike teams," I said. "I've heard about that, but I thought it was a rumor."

"Nope. And with John Gallows as my field leader, we can teleport them from anywhere to anywhere. I have heroes from all over the world with boots on the ground right now. Even several your government categorizes as criminals, such as Madjack."

Five minutes ago, Cobalt City had been in a panic. The locals had seen some shit in their time. They were used to the chaos the city's heroes and villains brought to life in the city. They might not always like it, but it was familiar. The dragons had pushed things into a new territory. It was too random. Too fantastical. It stretched the thresholds of believability.

And with Prather's anti-vigilante measures making it difficult for organized heroes and teams to operate, there had been a terrifying vacuum primed for something like this. Poised on the precipice, waiting for a failure of leadership to allow disaster to strike on a truly colossal scale.

But just like they always did when the city needed them, the heroes stood up. Not just to fight impossible creatures, but also to protect those in danger. To restore faith. To give hope in a seemingly hopeless situation.

And across the city, the tide began to turn.

"Madjack?" I asked. "I thought she was still on a terror watch list!"

"They're welcome to try and arrest her," Wrecker of Engines said. "But who isn't on a list these days? The good news is that if the King in Yellow was behind this to sow some kind of madness, I think it's backfiring."

"What makes you say that?"

"Well, for one, we're winning. And according to Madjack, the general emotional temperature as far as she can sense is hope. The city is resilient, Jacob. Those in power sought to bury us, but failed to realize we were seeds. Or something like that, at least. And we've given the city something to hope for."

I'll admit, I kind of hated the Wrecker of Engines simply on the basis of who he was and what he did. A hacker who could break into my systems seemingly at will scared the hell out of me. And Madjack, with her alien ability to read and manipulate emotions on a huge scale, well, that was a whole other level of terrifying. But he wasn't wrong. I could see the evidence of that myself across my news feeds, across the harvested social media data. Cobalt City is proud. It is stubborn. It is defiant.

And if an army of weird lizards thought they were going to defeat us, they were about to learn a difficult lesson.

"Where do you need me?"

"I've got a sludge dragon coming out of the service tunnels under the Cannonade. Kraken could use backup. I've put a pin in your GPS. When you're done there, the rest of Monster Squad might still need a hand at Mill Hill. I'll have Gallows port you over."

I stretched my back and cracked my knuckles. The pin appeared in the pin on my visor map. Two blocks east of William Blake Elementary. Piece of cake. "Tell Kraken I'm on my way."

My boot jets angled me down toward the old brick buildings of the Cannonade, where a young woman with shadowy tentacles sprouting from her back tussled with a sewer dragon in the middle of the street. I felt a huge smile spread across my face as across the city, we pushed back the threat, pushed back the fear. Together, we stood against the dark. Together, we were unstoppable.

I charged up a fresh pair of Starbolts and rocketed into the fray.

———

Nathan Crowder is an author, superhero geek, and award-winning karaoke singer living in the great Pacific Northwest. He has been frequently spotted in the rustic wilds southeast of Seattle poking around garden centers, talking to birds, or on the hunt for weird candy. He also once got in a fight with his much larger cousin over whether Green Arrow was a real superhero or not. Online, he resides on Twitter @NateCrowder or at www.NathanCrowder.com

Epilogue

by Nathan Crowder

From a high tower in distant Carcosa, the King in Yellow watched the storm of dragons flare up, only to be quashed one by one by one. For a time, for the briefest of moments, he had felt madness begin to overtake Cobalt City. The world had been a ripe, juicy plum, ready to be plucked. He felt the barriers between worlds flicker and weaken.

His visit to the Bazaar had taken too much of his personal energy. Stepping between worlds was not an easy affair, and it had costs. And while he suckled the rising insanity that trickled from Cobalt City and Iteration 5169, while it slaked his thirst, it had not been enough before his victory was tainted.

It had not been enough before the heroes, once thought beaten back to passivity by his long machinations with various agents of chaos, rallied to resist the dragonstorm.

The King in Yellow had hesitated. Too aware of his own limitations. Too cautious of the cost and blinded in many ways by the absence of his former agent and anchor Louis Malenfant. The mad fool had gone rogue, resisting his true purpose, and it had hindered the King in Yellow in ways he was not yet fully willing to accept.

The heroes of Cobalt City had brought hope in the world's moment of need. And that hope pushed back the shadows of doubt. Of fear. Of madness.

The conquest of this world would be even harder now. Harder, but not impossible. Madness, hopelessness, insanity, they always found a way to creep back in. Chaos was inevitable. And this world's resistance made the prospect of its inevitable downfall that much more delicious.

The King in Yellow reached out one impossible gnarled hand, fingertips grazing the barrier between worlds. He felt it weep sweet, sweet insanity.

It was a mad, mad, mad, mad world.

And soon.

Soon it would be his for the taking.

About the Artist

Luke Spooner, a.k.a. 'Carrion House,' currently lives and works in the South of England. Having recently graduated from the University of Portsmouth with a first class degree, he is now a full time illustrator for just about any project that piques his interest. Despite regular forays into children's books and fairy tales, his true love lies in anything macabre, melancholy, or dark in nature and essence. He believes that the job of putting someone else's words into a visual form, to accompany and support their text, is a massive responsibility, as well as being something he truly treasures. You can visit his web site at www.carrionhouse.com.

www.ingramcontent.com/pod-product-compliance
Lightning Source LLC
Chambersburg PA
CBHW060942120626
46557CB00003B/1105